I0741495

WORD Walkers

Muyomreshi
250 miles
Domgat
Salli
ORIMBELA
Mundang
IRONBORN EM
Saibala
Moago
Okonle
Javtont
Akoda
Duwe
Bayavite N
Moenum
DRAKKON
KALMARAN
Komonikon
Kalvari
Marinhede
MYSTHAL
Civivento
Moschato
Amaso
PLED

N
ASTLOR
HANMARK
ENDRA
RUTHUN
Battgana
Magangrad
Duzuscow
Tambonetsk
Nianapa
Iivangow
Novotroik
Havas
Sevavda
Graen
Menbrook
Enburn
Vinhir
Westcreek
Hawkfel
Manarfell
Dane
Cornhal
Clifcaster
Gosmire
Blöngarás
bling
ang

Edited by Danielle Rich & Bobbie Jo Reid

Map by Taegen J. Murphy

ISBN 978-1-7335826-1-2

BOOK 1:

STOLEN SECRET

By Amelia C. M. Moseley

For Mrs. Wanda Wilds.

*I would never have gotten here without you
pushing me forward.*

Thank you.

PROLOGUE

Where is Dau'fi?

The thought fleeted quickly as the fighter moved to parry the blow aimed at her. She blocked, letting the blade grind across hers before moving to counter. Gravel skidded under her foot as she moved into the next move in the fight. Another parry, another swing, another dodge. A routine warm-up, one that pulled on every muscle and memory in her.

Along the sides of the training arena knelt a handful of other figures. Long, slender ears twitched, tilting to and fro at even the smallest sounds. They watched the fighters, comments held until the end of

the match. As she skirted her opponent's attack, she did her best to ignore them. Yet she found their expressions important. Notes of approval or distain, silent bets on the scene before them.

Another swing plunged her attention back into the fight. Sweep, dodge, thrust, counter. She buried herself in her actions, concentrating with renewed determination. She became so focused on the clash of metal, the flow of battle, the rhythm of their dance, that all else melted away. Even the sounds of the garden around them faded away, birdsong a distant whisper.

Until one voice cut through the din.

"Kan'sa."

The female Hantheer blinked, her deer-like ears swiveling toward the speaker. Both her and her opponent bowed, the match over at the entrance of their master. As Kan'sa's partner joined the others on the edge of the field, she smiled at the voice's owner, "Master Dau'fi." It was only as she approached her master that she realized what he had said. She looked up, her eyes connecting with her elder, unable to hide the brief flash of surprise in her reddish-brown eyes. Kan'*sa*.

Master Dau'fi smiled in return, but Kan'sa saw the crease in his brow, the pain on his lips, the pride in his eyes. She pressed her lips together, guessing what he was about to say, but stopping herself from interrupting him. Master Dau'fi swallowed, hiding his emotions quickly for his following announcement: "Kan'sa, the Speaker has chosen you as their World Walker."

Those words. Those were the words Kan'sa had been training her whole life to hear. There were very few Hantheer chosen to be trained for the position, but even fewer were chosen to actually take up the mantle of World Walker. The title came with its own horrible weight, its own heavy responsibility. Peace often came at a high price, a price the World Walker would need to bear alone with no help from their home or deity. That *she* would have to bear alone.

"What darkness is approaching the Speaker's mortal world?" Kan'sa asked, stepping beside her master as he motioned for her. As she did, she saw her companions rise, all bowing to her with a new kind of respect. It was a formal gesture, one that some of the younger Hantheer in the audience didn't quite grasp. Kan'sa tucked away thoughts of leaving her peers behind as she and Dau'fi walked away from the arena and over the wooden walkway toward the heart of their city.

"You should know by now that we know nothing about what approaches, only that it comes," Master Dau'fi answered. He turned his head, concentrating on the walkway ahead of them. His mentorship had been more than a student-teacher relationship for them both. They had had centuries together, now to be torn apart for Speaker knew how long. Dau'fi had been many things for Kan'sa. Part of her worried about being in the mortal world without his guidance, but now was not the time for fear. She was chosen. She could not let her people believe she would fail.

Kan'sa set her hand on her mentor's shoulder, resolved in her mask. "There is no one who could have prepared me better for this life, Master. I will conquer whatever is troubling these lands."

Master Dau'fi pressed his hand against hers and nodded. "Come, there is much to discuss and little time before you go."

The two walked side-by-side through the open-air halls of Fahla'surni, home of the Hantheer, talking softly about Kan'sa's responsibilities, but not the task itself. They walked on the wooden bridges raised over the many gardens and training arenas around Kan'sa's home, through the spiderweb of businesses laced between stone gardens and parks. At the sight of the two, others stepped aside. It didn't take long for the city to start chatting about the newly chosen World Walker; the gossip spilled over the bridges running parallel to Kan'sa and Dau'fi. Crowds began to gather, bowing to Kan'sa. She waved meekly, trying to stow her emotions. She was to be a leader, to bring peace to another world. She wouldn't leave her people worrying whether she would succeed.

Master Dau'fi led Kan'sa to a platform that overlooked the city. Trees mingled with wooden buildings. The bridges and buildings came together like beads on a great woven tapestry, the gardens filling the squares between. Mist still clung to the rooftops as the morning was chased away by the sun. "The Speaker will guide you through all things. Remember your training, all that you have learned. Do not fear to ask for aid, but do not allow fear of the unknown guide you. We are a blessed race, but we are not perfect. Or immortal. But we are still a symbol. And now you are their symbol. You cannot let them believe you think this evil will stop you."

Whether he meant her own people or the mortals she was being sent to save, she didn't know. Kan'sa nodded. "I will remember all of this."

The elder Hantheer tried to laugh, but the noise was caught in his throat. He turned toward Kan'sa. "Your companion is being told. Kil'thian will follow you shortly when you call for him.

"As your master, I am supposed to provide you a gift. Traditionally a weapon is given, but I have elected for something else. In hopes that you will go to bring peace, not war. Perhaps an end to this cycle. I give this small bit of knowledge around our rules that it may aid you in a quest where your people nor your divine may answer you."

He clasped Kan'sa's hands as the mist began to rise, moving from where it rested, and began swirling before them on their platform to form a crack between worlds. "Find Vinhir. Find the war that happened there over a week."

Kan'sa pondered the statement as the portal ripped open behind her. "Master, I don't—"

Master Dau'fi folded his arms and stepped away. He could aid her no more, such were the laws of the World Walker. Beyond help of her people, beyond true answers from her deity. Only she could discover her path forward now. Kan'sa bowed in respect to her mentor. His expression was beginning to falter, but Kan'sa wouldn't allow him to suffer through more farewells. She turned toward the portal. It was as if the world had been ripped in two. Tendrils of nowhereness lashed out as the world fought to put itself back together. What was beyond the rift was incomprehensible, appearing as little more than a blinding mist.

For a moment, Kan'sa looked back. She frowned at herself at this confession of weakness, but she tore herself from the spot. She rushed to her master's side, grasping him in a tight embrace. "I cannot lie, Master, I am afraid."

Dau'fi ran a hand through her hair. She felt hot tears on her face, both her own and her friend's. She heard him reciting the Speaker's word and smiled. "Fear not, my child. For I am the way and the truth. I will always guide you, even when you cannot understand my path. Know me and you will never fail."

Kan'sa pushed back, her arms still tangled with Dau'fi's. His own mask had fallen, a small, bittersweet smile on his face. But his lips remained pressed together. He had said too much. Kan'sa could see pleading in his eyes, begging their deity to let him comfort her further, but Dau'fi remained silent.

Heavy-hearted, Kan'sa stepped back. She blinked once, the tears falling away from her face. Then, she passed through the tear in the world before it righted reality behind her.

Her skin prickled. She felt her flesh turn to mist and then back to flesh and then to mist again, over and over as she passed through the barriers that separated worlds. She closed her eyes as the transformations became blinding and unreality undid reality and then doubled back upon itself.

And then, it stopped. She felt whole again. Kan'sa blinked her eyes open, looking up to see the sun and the dark woods that surrounded her. She thanked the Speaker that the mist had stung her whole skin, turning it all a prickled red and hiding her tears.

Her ears swiveled forward, sent toward a new speaker.

"What the hell just happened?"

Kan'sa looked down, her head spinning a little at the sharp movement. She hadn't adjusted yet. She studied the speaker for a moment as her head corrected itself. A dwarf woman stood before her, the shock on her face plain to see. The poor woman was almost white, though, for an individual of a primarily subterranean race, that didn't seem like a hard feat. Around them were a dozen scorch marks on stones and trees littering the glade.

To Vinhir then, Kan'sa thought. Keeping her face masked, she spoke, "Greetings. My name is Kan'sa of Fahla'surni, and I am the World Walker. Would you like to go on an adventure?"

Silence.

Kan'sa coughed, her fist covering her

lips. She offered again. "I come on a quest of great importance for this world."

Still nothing.

"It's a holy quest, and I am in need of aid."

Finally, the dwarf began to move. She furrowed her brow, shaking her head. Kan'sa smiled as the conversation was going to start making progress. Kan'sa opened her mouth to explain further, but the dwarf spoke first:

"What the fuck?"

CHAPTER 1
THE HART WANTS WHAT THE HART WANTS

Diana shrugged her pack onto her shoulders. They were in the middle of nowhere, but she didn't really have a right to complain. She signed up for this, however stupid the idea was. She'd taken her strange new companion's proposition without hesitation or further questions. Not that she was fond of staying where she was. Dane was a miserable town. She'd been waiting years for a reason to put it behind her.

Kan'sa took long, even strides in front of her. Everything about the woman screamed power and grace. And tall, taller than any mortal race Diana knew. Long strands of tawny hair bounced against her back, sheltering a lean, freckled face and black doe's nose. Soft would likely have been someone's first impression of seeing Kan'sa, but closer analysis showed hard angles. A gentle giant, but there was no doubt this woman was a warrior. She was conscious of Diana's limitations, and kept her pace set slower, slow enough to keep from making Diana run while making sure they still made decent time.

"So, Vinhir?" Diana asked, finally working up the nerve to break the silence.

STOLEN SECRET

Ever since she had agreed to come along,
she had been scared to talk to the woman.
What if Kan'sa thought she was crazy now?
After all, it's not every day that folks sell
their apartment so they can go on epic
quests with strangers who say they're from
beyond known reality. But something in
Diana wouldn't let her turn Kan'sa down,
beyond wanting to leave Dane.
Encountering Kan'sa had been like meeting
a friend who Diana had always known and
then finally seeing them again for the first
time in years. It didn't make sense to Diana,
but she couldn't shake the feeling once it
dawned on her. So here she was. Wherever
that might lead. Thoughts of grand
adventures lingered in her mind for seconds
before fleeting. Did Kan'sa think Diana
would be any good at that, adventuring? Or

maybe Kan'sa was just a good salesperson and needed a redemption story to sell. Diana wasn't entirely sure at this point, but even as she was uncertain about moving forward, she was confident she didn't want to go back.

"That is my goal," Kan'sa answered, "though first I would like to summon my companion. He will make travel much easier."

"And this is a hart, right?"

Kan'sa nodded as she kept walking. Diana looked around—trying to find a distinguishing feature in the woods—but trees were trees to her. There wasn't an evergreen that stood out to her, so she just kept walking, trusting that Kan'sa had a better sense of direction. Hopefully, after they had summoned Kan'sa's mount, they would be returning to the roads. Diana felt more comfortable on a defined path, but maybe that was because she was so used to traveling in the Underway, not on the surface. Though even her days on the dwarven highway were distant to her now.

Calling the roads "roads" between Dane and Vinhir would have been an overstatement. They were little more than glorified hunting trails in most places, with the brush poorly hacked away to make room for carts. While they were decently well marked, they were certainly not paved. Maybe someone had thought to add some loose stones to the paths that had dug into the dirt from being tread on so often. At least the soil was soft under her feet.

They had been walking for a day. Diana had brought the rest of her food, all her scrolls and magic theory notes, clothing, and anything else she thought was particularly important, which wasn't much. She may have been leaving her home behind, but that didn't mean she was giving up her research.

Diana gave most of the money she had gotten from selling her home to Kan'sa, since the woman had appeared with nothing but the clothes on her back. Kan'sa had bartered a huntsman's bow and a small hunting knife from a trader, and they had left Dane behind. Diana wasn't sad to leave though. She thought she might have been, but after a day of hiking, she was thinking more about Vinhir than Dane. And about her mysterious new companion. The woman continued ahead, ignorant of Diana's infrequent glances.

STOLEN SECRET

At about dusk, Kan'sa found a spot to sleep. It wasn't more than an outcrop of rocks, but at least if it rained, they would have some shelter. Diana sat down against the stones as her companion went about building a fire. It had been two days now since they had met, since she had agreed to follow Kan'sa along, since Kan'sa had mentioned her hart, but still, nothing had appeared.

"When were you going to summon your deer again?" she asked, fishing through Kan'sa's bag for something to eat, as if travel tack was a real food. They had decided that it may be better to keep the food in Kan'sa's pack, away from Diana's scrolls and paper. Ink wasn't exactly a cheap commodity, and neither of them had a real trade at the moment.

"When he is ready."

"Doesn't summoning work the other way around? The summoner summons when they are ready, right?"

"Perhaps," Kan'sa answered, "but I am not summoning a spirit or a creature. I am summoning a friend, and so he should be able to come on his own time. Even then, Kil'thian is unique, even among his kind. I fully believe he would refuse me if I asked him when he was not ready to leave. However, I trust he will respect my summons tonight. He's had quite enough time to say his goodbyes."

"He certainly sounds interesting."

Their campfire sputtered and then danced to life. The flitting embers replaced the setting sun as Kan'sa sat down beside Diana and began to eat part of their ration of bread.

"Kil'thian is, certainly. I do not know why the Speaker sent him to me, but I would not trade his companionship for the world. Of course, he has been mine since I was small, and centuries of friendship tend to cause such deep attachments."

"Still, Vinhir is a long hike. How long until he's ready?"

"When he is, he will be," Kan'sa answered calmly, "but more than that, I cannot tell. I can only ask, and hope he answers."

Diana considered asking more questions but elected to turn to her notes. Kan'sa had just stepped into a new world with information that didn't even scratch the surface of her quest's needs based on the questions Diana had managed to ask before selling her plot. Why are you here? What are you doing? Where are you going? To save the world. Specifically, I can't say. Vinhir, to investigate a civil war.

Diana barely knew anything about dwarven politics, much less anything about Daendran politics. She wasn't even certain which war Kan'sa needed, or if there was some other conflict altogether she was looking for on the horizon. The conversation she had with Kan'sa when they first met covered the bare minimum of a civil war that happened eighty years ago in the capital, and most of it she only knew from dealing with agitated traders tired of the taxes the ruling family had implemented afterward.

"What if your task is a civil war here now?" Diana asked. "There is a lot of rebellion going on in the kingdom. No one can hold on to Daendra. The last king couldn't, and King Arvon has a very loose grasp now."

"It's possible," Kan'sa replied. "Though that would be a very small thing to change, too small for a World Walker. Unless Daendra went on a great campaign after a new king was seated, I do not know if that would fulfill my role. But I suppose only the Speaker knows, and so will I when my job is done. I think Vinhir is a good place to start though, both for this notion of war and for helping me understand the current history."

"There's also a pretty big oratory in Hawkfel, which I think is on the way. If you wanted to speak to a priest, perhaps they could help you sort things out. I don't really know much about history topside. Only been up here thirty-ish years."

"That is a fair point, though I did not expect you to suggest speaking to someone of the faith."

"Why not?" Diana inquired. Sure, she probably didn't go to Dane's oratory as much as she ought to, but she believed in the Speaker—that there was one, at least.

"Just how many times you took the Speaker's name in vain when we met would suggest that you don't put much weight in their power. I'm surprised to hear that you believe in the Spoken Truth."

"That's—" Diana started, scratching the back of her head as she felt her face burn. "A bad habit. But if I talked like a clergy, I'd never have kept my doors open. Don't trust the cloth for fair deals."

Kan'sa frowned for a moment before her expression softened. "That is a sad truth, but I will not ask you to change your habits. I do not believe you truly mean to insult the Speaker by saying it." The Hantheer looked away, musing about something as she gazed over the forest, "We all could use more guidance from them, after all."

Diana turned her head, feeling like she was in someone's morning oratory lesson. "Right." She shifted awkwardly, not sure if she'd just been reprimanded by Kan'sa, someone who was nearly a stranger, or if this was something she should expect from someone calling themselves the World Walker.

The Hantheer raised her hands as she twisted back to face Diana. "Do not trouble yourself for me. It is your faith and your words. That is between you and the Speaker. I'm sure I will become used to it if it is a common trader's practice."

A silence grew between them. Diana tried to scribble out runes for her most recent spell project. Kan'sa broke it eventually. "I suppose it makes taking notes difficult, losing the scrolls once you activate them? It is a craft that seems to encourage perfection or hasty decisions."

"Not making mistakes is the important part for my wallet," Diana answered, with a laugh. "I make a duplicate in my journal before I write it out on the scroll. Saves time on trying to figure out what went wrong."

"I have never been able to study enchanting, my people put little focus in the arcane," Kan'sa stated. "How does it work?"

"You shoot mana into a series of coded runes, generally speaking, and hope you don't blow up," Diana answered. "It's like a word puzzle. I'm decent at them, despite the, you know, the magical limitations." Dwarven immunity to magic certainly proved a hurdle for being a mage. "Manastones help get over that limitation though, supposing I can find someone to charge them for me."

"I see."

"I just do minor enchantments, so that's about all I can say," Diana finished. She held up the completed scroll. "I've done this one before, it should be fine. I'll save it for when we need a sudden lightning bolt."

"Scroll writing is an under-practiced art." Kan'sa tilted her head back, a sign

Diana had gathered meant the Hantheer was searching for some bit of knowledge. "I do not believe many outside the High Seat practice it, not only because of its time and money commitment. What inspired you to study such an unexplored craft?"

"I wanted to be a mage. I always joked about it when I was a kid, about being able to do the impossible, I guess. Now I'm an adult with my own income, so I figured I might give it another try," Diana replied. "I can't create magic on my own, but I figure I can cheat the rules a little. I can figure out the wording easy enough, manastones can do the rest. Besides, nothing beats a rough day like figuring out how to tighten a mass of fire into a column of death." Diana grinned a little, jotting down a note on the side of her journal.

Kan'sa was silent for a while. The Hantheer leaned her head back against the stone face and closed her eyes. Diana fidgeted with her notes, sorting them back into her pack. As the fire died down, Kan'sa finally spoke again, "I believe you and Kil'thian will get along quite well."

Diana curled up in her bedroll, staring at the stars above her. Kan'sa sat beside her in a meditative state. That was the closest to sleeping Kan'sa seemed to get. Here she was, out in the middle of nowhere, camping with a stranger. All number of things could go horribly wrong, but turning back now would be humiliating. She had committed to this adventure and sold her apartment just to try it. She couldn't turn back now, not two days after she had left. She had to make it somewhere first.

Diana rolled over, drawing her blanket over her. For the first time in a long time, she felt small, or at least, was aware that she did. She knew dwarves were supposed to be miniature miners with huge halls to compensate, but she had never felt small in Dane or in the few other dwarven cities she had visited. Kan'sa was considerate of Diana's height in a non-condescending way, so that wasn't it. Or maybe it was. The thought of someone willingly going out of their way to consider Diana's height was new. Either she had lived with dwarves or lived with humans who didn't give two shits.

She pulled her pack closer to her, feeling it sink under her grasp. This was all she had left of her old life. Why did she decide to give it up? For magic and scrolls?

That was certainly exciting to consider, but no. Was it wanderlust? Kan'sa had baited her into this whole thing by suggesting Diana had it, by asking her to go on an adventure.

Rolling onto her back, Diana searched the stars. Dwarves didn't have names for constellations, not when they lived underground. Diana didn't know any of those names now. She wondered if the dirin or the Hantheer gave them names. Maybe even the dragonkin found names for the heavens in their reclusive settlements beyond the civilized world.

In the end, she decided that she felt small because it had finally dawned on her how big the world was and how little she had really done in it. The conversation in her head was getting too philosophical, so she decided to go to sleep.

Dawn hit her with its dew and sunlight. Diana groaned as she sat up. She would probably never get used to sleeping outdoors. She looked forward to Kan'sa figuring out whatever it was she was supposed to be doing here, on her quest. Diana was starting to think Kan'sa was an excellent salesperson because Diana had agreed to come along while barely remembering anything Kan'sa had actually said about this quest. Kan'sa didn't seem to know much about that matter herself. I should ask about that, she mused, shaking the sleep from her eyes.

Diana hoped more though that Kan'sa would not be opposed to offerings for her holy services. Right now, coin was a non-renewable resource.

The camp was empty. Diana looked around, but everything was gone. Well, perhaps not everything. Kan'sa and their fire had disappeared. Diana was still neatly tucked away under the stone outcropping. The pack by her side said Kan'sa was not a thief, but she was still gone.

Diana rolled up her bedding and pulled her pack onto her back. She had no idea where the nearest road was either, so getting anywhere was going to be a pain.

A bugle reverberated through the forest. Diana covered her ears, searching for what could have made the sound. There was no chance that an elk would be this close. They would smell her or the remains of the fire, surely, and avoid the camp.

Then she saw him. Diana didn't

hunt, but she knew the difference between a stag and a hart the moment she laid eyes on him. He practically glided across the ground, with power and muscle unlike any creature in this world. His tawny pelt glimmered in the sunrise, the black along his spine glossy and smooth. The same color reached down as a shaggy mane beneath his head and ebony fur feathering above his hooves. Like the branches of a barren stone oak, his antlers towered up into a briar of hard antlers as black as onyx.

An elk may be lord to a forest of deer, but a hart is the true king of all woods. And as that mighty beast approached Diana in the clearing, she finally understood why oratories preached that deer were signs from the Speaker.

Diana felt her knees go weak. She

managed at least, "You're Kil'thian." The words came out clearly, despite the hairs rising on the back of Diana's neck.

The hart snorted, shaking his massive head. He towered above Diana as he approached. He bent down, snorting again. The breath hit Diana like a hot summer wind. She met his amber eyes, bright like wildfire.

"You're really something else," Diana said, the awe apparent in her voice. Kil'thian jostled his head as
if he already knew. "A little vain, there, huh?"

Kil'thian huffed loudly and raised his head, though he continued to watch her for a moment in curiosity. He turned, looking deeper into the woods. Diana followed his eyes, searching for whatever he was searching for, praying it was Kan'sa. She turned back to the hart. "Where is she?"

The hart didn't break his stare from the deeper woods. He stepped forward once, twice, bringing himself adjacent to Diana. Then, he dropped to his knees. He slowly turned to face Diana again, those eyes connecting once more with hers. Diana blinked. "You want me to ride you?"

He huffed again, letting her know that was obvious. Diana grunted back at him, the little princeling. "All right, all right, mighty stag o' the Speaker, I get it." And Kan'sa said they'd get along.

Diana pulled herself up onto his back. She had never ridden before, but she had seen plenty of traders do it. Surely a hart was similar to a horse. He seemed to laugh. Diana would have grumbled back if she hadn't been worried about being thrown off this huge creature. What a fall off a horse was for a human or an elf was a little riskier for a dwarf. And this was no horse.

As Diana twisted her fingers into Kil'thian's mane, the hart stood. Diana pressed her knees down, though she was already stretching pretty far as it was to spread her legs across the wide seat of the beast. Without waiting to make sure Diana was holding on, Kil'thian started forward. She leaned in, pressing down against the hart's neck.

How Kil'thian knew where he was going, Diana didn't know. She trusted it was because of whatever bond he and Kan'sa shared. He flew through the woods, smooth as a trained gaited horse. Fortunately, he didn't jump. Diana felt like she would have been launched off if he decided to do that. But as she kept her head pressed forward, she missed the woods blurring past as Kil'thian sailed on.

The hart slowed after a while, turning to look down the hill. Diana followed his gaze. Kan'sa stood opposite three men wearing the crest of the king, all brandishing swords to face Kan'sa's bow. Her quiver, however, appeared largely featherless beside the arrow drawn now. They leered at her, making Diana's skin crawl. Kan'sa was backed against a fence, searching for a way out as the three guardsmen marched forward.

Shoving a hand into her pack, Diana shouted, "Hey, get away from her, assholes!"

One looked up at her, pointed with his sword, and his companions followed suit as he hollered, "Or what, stoneheart?" Diana pressed her lips together hard into a thin line at the slur. "You'll come down off your big deer and kick our shins? This is royal business. Stay out of it."

Kil'thian snorted, his fur ruffling at being called a deer. Diana leaned forward slightly as she grasped a scroll. "How do you feel about burning them alive?"

The hart quivered his approval as Diana felt for the wax seal on her scrolls. A fire spell. Hopefully a working one. Diana felt her lips dry as she shouted back, "How about you let my friend go before I light everything in your chest cavity on fire?"

The guard laughed. "What, you think you can use magic, stoneheart? Did you fall down one of your mine shafts and suddenly think you were a mage?"

Diana swallowed. She'd never actually used one of her spells on something before. Not living at least. There were scorched stones all around Dane from her tests, but no living person had ever been her target. Could she really do this?

Yes, she could. She could defend herself. Soldiers killed all the time. What was the difference here? She could do this.

Kil'thian pushed forward. His steady canter made ground, but Diana knew he had no intention of running himself on those rusted short swords. She was going to do this, whether she liked it or not.

"Kil'thian, stay out of this," Kan'sa barked. It was the first time Diana heard her be harsh, but it didn't stop the hart.

Diana's nail cut the scroll's seal. She wasn't going to sit idle behind Kan'sa.

Kan'sa was giving her a chance to see the world, to study magic, to be part of something bigger, to make a difference. Diana had given up everything for this moment, to be part of this adventure, and she was not going to let Kan'sa fight alone.

Diana was not going to be small.

She felt the energy snap in her hand as the scroll consumed itself. It glanced off Diana's palm but did not seep in. Magic cannot exist inside a dwarf. Kil'thian turned to give Diana the shot. She extended her palm out toward the guards to throw the spell and–

Nothing.

The energy sputtered in her palm and vanished. Diana swore, "Speaker's fucking Will, not a dud, not now, dammit—"

A spear of lightning crashed through

the trees. Even Kil'thian jumped back a pace as the spell hit the guard who had spoken. The figure spasmed and died, wisps of electricity still coursing off him as he collapsed.

There was silence. The guards didn't move. Kan'sa was stock still. Diana blinked, feeling bile rising in her throat. She had just...just...

Kil'thian looked back at her, his eyes asking her what she planned to do next. Diana swallowed down the rising burning in her throat, roaring, "You two want to say hello to the Speaker with or without the help of a priest next?"

Without another word, they fled, scrambling back into the woods, the sound of rattling armor fading quickly in the distance. Kan'sa relaxed as they vanished into the distance. Diana let go of her breath. And her dinner.

The hart was not pleased about Diana losing her meal. He promptly bounced her off his back at the insult, though Kan'sa, probably seeing this coming, took two strides to catch Diana as she fell.

"I pray that that never gets easier, my friend," Kan'sa said, setting Diana down. "Though I hope you will be able to keep your stomach if it happens again."

Diana took a moment to breathe as Kan'sa handed her their waterskin. She drank slowly until her stomach settled.

"I'm afraid I do not know the meaning of the insult they threw at you. I will not use it, but having a stone heart," she was conscious to pause between the words, "seems like it would say that an individual has a particularly strong resolve.”

“Maybe that’s what it meant when your last World Walker was here,” Diana answered, trying to hide the bitterness she had gotten so used to explaining why the term was not all right. She shook her head, letting out a sigh. “But I’ve…it’s a slur against dwarves. Let’s leave it at that.”

“I am sorry then,” Kan’sa replied. “Still, you were very brave. That was an impressive scroll. Was that the one you wrote last night?”

Diana nodded, still surprised to have pulled it off. She looked into the woods. “Should we be worried about the other two?”

“I doubt it,” Kan’sa said. After a moment, she answered Diana’s silent question, “I saw the Daendran crest on their tunics and thought they might be able to inform me more about the current state of affairs here. It appears I was wrong."

"Nothing good comes out of the king's guards. They're largely bandits these days, making up fake taxes on traveling merchants," Diana grumbled. She took a deep breath as a grim thought came to mind. "I guess we'll have a bounty on our heads next time we go into town."

Kan'sa clasped her chin, musing for a moment before shaking her head in disagreement. "They seemed persistent, but I doubt they will report this officially to any town. They would be too worried about the rumors that might spread from it, which would be a touch unbelievable for most."

"Like what?"

"Why, a dwarf who can wield magic,

riding in on a hart of legend," Kan'sa answered, gesturing to Kil'thian, who was still bitter about Diana throwing up. "After all, the oratories say that harts are the messengers of the Speaker."

Diana thought about the comment. Kil'thian shook his head, reading something Diana didn't know. Diana looked away, not wanting to pick the Hantheer's brain on whatever it was that Kan'sa was beaming about. "Well, that would be quite the rumor. Wonder what they'll say in Vinhir when you arrive."

Kan'sa smiled. "I'm sure it will impress."

CHAPTER 2
HAWKFEL, THE CITY OF OVERZEALOUS PRIESTS AND OPEN REBELLIONS

Hawkfel was out of the way to Vinhir. It veered off to the west while the road to Vinhir turned to the east. At the fork in the road, the party had added two days to their travel on route to Hawkfel. The decision had come down to Diana needing a real bed over the knotted forest floor. Kan'sa agreed since she wanted to hear more rumors, possibly about the guards, but more about the rebellion brewing in the winds in Daendra. And Hawkfel didn't seem to hide its rebellious spirit. Traders they passed spoke about it blatantly, some suggesting the lord was about to hold a feast in the name of such a rebellion. Any hope of support for the guards had fallen on unwilling ears.

Calling Hawkfel a city was an overstatement. Hawkfel was an old fort with a village cropped up around it. It sat atop a rocky shelf, with a higher ridge hugging the fort's back walls. A few businesses sat on the cliffs, but most of them coiled down the road through the village. There was a lot of farmland close to the shelf, though the rocky ground produced more sheep pens than crops. With the mountains to the southeast, and the dense woods surrounding the rest of their borders, Hawkfel held a defensible position.

Diana sat in front of Kan'sa on Kil'thian's back as they rode toward the edges of Hawkfel. The hart had begrudgingly let her ride him, and by the time they reached Hawkfel, he seemed to have stopped holding the scene with the guards against her. For now, at least. In any case, riding in front of Kan'sa meant she had better support. Kil'thian didn't have a saddle, so at least the Hantheer gave Diana something to hold on to if the hart tried to throw her.

As they strode among the farmhouses, Diana leaned around Kil'thian's broad neck to get a view of the fort. Its stone walls were inelegant and rough but sturdy. Daendran-made. There was no way a dwarf would allow that kind of building to stand, not with its unsmoothed walls or jagged supports sticking out. Still, the fort did have a kind of rugged beauty to it. It stood defiant and absolute against the wild. She had heard too many times that that represented the people here as well, though she had never seen that side of Daendra in Dane. Hawkfel was the kind of place typical in Daendran folk stories. Perhaps these rumors of a rebellion were another in a set of tall tales from the village.

Townspeople watched as they rode into the town proper. They paused their work, commenting on the scene as if the visitors couldn't hear them.

"Is that really a hart?"

"Does this mean the Speaker is against the king too? I don't imagine

Frederick will need a better sign than that if they are."

"Speaker's Will, are they going to bring us a new king?"

Diana leaned back behind Kil'thian's neck. "You know how to make an entrance."

Kan'sa murmured to Diana, "I would be careful being so prominent, or they might think similarly of you."

"Well, they would be wrong. It's a long fall from Killy, here, and I'd rather not have to jump off, so you can have the spotlight."

Kil'thian snorted, discontent with the nickname. Kan'sa patted his side and pulled him to a halt. "Perhaps we should make less of a scene of ourselves." She tapped her heels against Kil'thian's sides and the hart knelt. Diana was grateful for the action. She knew Kan'sa could dismount Kil'thian without having him bend down, but Diana did not want to get assistance while they were the center of attention.

Diana shifted her books around in her pack as Kan'sa stroked her hart. "Find somewhere safe, friend, and I will call for you soon. Hunters may know you, but bears will not."

Kil'thian nodded his head before he bugled softly. Then he turned and raced down the road back toward the forests beyond Hawkfel. Kan'sa tightened her pack and turned to Diana. "Ready then?"

"As I'll ever be," Diana answered.

The chatter followed them as they got closer to the center of Hawkfel, whispers about the hart that came and went, the deer elf and her short companion, and the lord who needed a sign from the heavens for his feast. A conversation between two wash maids caught Diana's attention.

"Wickers said he saw a dwarf cast a lightning spell the other day. You think that's her?"

"Dwarves can't cast magic, don't you know?"

"What do you think then? A demon did it and crawled up in a dwarf's skin?"

"Can't be no demon, not in the company of a hart like that."

"Suppose that's true."

The houses clustered together tighter the further they went, and shops along the road became more frequent. The only inn in town, they were told, sat at the top of the rocky cliff before the fort, but it didn't do much in the way of food. At least not until the evening.

Instead of waiting for a hot meal, Diana and Kan'sa elected to slip into a pub house to have something to eat besides dried meat and travel tack. This was the longest Diana had gone without clean water, despite the efforts she and Kan'sa had made. She looked forward to a drink that wasn't chased by stagnation.

"The Hunter's Pleasure," Kan'sa read as they took a seat in the tavern. "I suppose I should send another prayer for Kil'thian."

"Are you worried about him?" Diana asked. She paused, adding half under her breath, "I mean, about him being hunted."

"Normally, no. But considering how much of a sight the both of us are, I can't assume these hunters will know perfectly what Kil'thian is. I will ask the priests when we visit the oratory here," Kan'sa decided.

"What are oratories like in Fahla'surni?" Diana asked, making eye contact with one of the barmaids and raising her hand to get her attention.

"Since I have not been to one in Daendra, or in all of this world, for that matter, I cannot tell you how they are different beyond what my mentor told me," Kan'sa explained as the barmaid approached their table, "but we hold our sermons outside, led by our priest caste."

"So, you're the funny looking elf everyone has been talkin' about?" the woman asked, the drawl in her voice hitting the word "elf" with a brief tension.

"I am a Hantheer, not an elf," Kan'sa answered calmly. She'd given the same relaxed explanation to Diana when they met, and then to the half a dozen travelers they'd met since.

"Yeah, love, and I'm the Blessed. We have rabbit for lunch, but there's ale and mead on tap. No beer until the evening, little lady," the barmaid explained, smiling as if what she said was considerate. Diana didn't have time to explain why that assumption was insulting.

"Whichever is stronger," Diana said, trying to hide her bite about the beer comment. If she was going to have to deal with more assuming humans, she needed it.

Kan'sa leaned in, stating, "The mead, but lunch for us both."

"'Course."

Diana refused to watch the woman leave and focused on the center of the table. This place reeked, and she was tired of being the only dwarf anyone had ever met. But that was going to be her lot in this adventure. Dwarves didn't go further than their mines unless they had a contract to build something.

"I'm glad we've heard nothing about those guards," Kan'sa commented, obviously trying more than Diana to avoid scrunching up her nose at the smell of the place. Diana had been to worse pubs along the Underway, but the stench of travelers and horses here hung to the wood frame like a curse.

"Agreed," Diana answered. "That was an untested scroll. I thought it was going to be a fireball when I broke the wax."

"How fortunate that it was mislabeled then," Kan'sa mused as the barmaid came back with their drinks and the shallow bowls of seared rabbit. The smell of onions and garlic blocked out the smell of the stables for a moment, but the broth was watery, and the seasoning was about all the flavor in the meal.

But the ale was decent.

Diana could get stronger alcohol in Dane, and dwarves never watered-down beer, no matter what it cost to keep it stocked. The ale had a good enough bite that it helped Diana calm her temper from dealing with the barmaid. She finished the pint and waited on Kan'sa, who was slow to finish, eager to listen and observe the life around her, whether she found it pleasant or not. The Hantheer sipped her tankard of mead as if it was a goblet of wine.

Diana looked down at her empty drink, swirling the last remains as she piped up, "I suppose this will be fairly common from here on out, yeah?"

"At least it's a step above dried and salted," Kan'sa answered, laughing lightly as she sipped the mead.

"Barely," Diana said, chuckling. "Hopefully the inn is nicer."

"Inns usually are, but at a cost," Kan'sa countered. "At the moment, we are unemployed."

"Surely the World Walker can fix that."

Kan'sa took another sip from her mug before answering, "The Blessed may fund me if I visit her, but there is a chance that she may also see us as acting against the Speaker until my quest bears results. That has happened to World Walkers before me, being contested by the leader of the

Spoken Truth. That said, we should still consider alternative options for funding until I can find proof of my quest, or even a direction I can guarantee. And that first leads us to Vinhir before Hanmark."

"What do you suggest?"

"We are traveling, so trapping may be beneficial, but that is only a limited amount of income and requires us to remain near forests," Kan'sa went on, "So a more scholarly profession may do us well once we near Vinhir, and the woods are less common. We have time to consider it, but we *should* consider it."

Diana leaned back in her seat, letting the thought roll around in her head. She could do enchantments, but manastones cost money, and time. Those were easier when you had a shop to work in. And asking for a wagon that could provide some workspace also required money—for the wagon and an animal to pull it. Speaker knew Kil'thian would never agree to be a beast of burden like that. They technically had the coin for it, barely, but Diana didn't know how she felt about handing over all of it so quickly. Kan'sa had spent most of it, leaving them with only a handful for food and rest when they passed through towns.

They left some coins on the table and walked out. Outside, the street was empty. Not even the farmers were still looking on from their yards to gossip about Diana and Kan'sa. The two exchanged a glance, before they took to the edge of the road to continue their progress toward the oratory.

As they approached the bend in the road that started the climb to the top of

Hawkfel, a rider came thundering down toward them. The rider charged past them, turning hard around the bend, and continued out of the city.

"Who do you think that was?" Kan'sa asked.

"Looked like a courier of some kind," Diana answered as they continued up the hill. She looked down and saw residents slowly leaving their homes. "Curious business, Hawkfel."

"The two of you wouldn't have happened to see a rider pass through here?"

Diana turned around to face the speaker. She had to remember to look up. The woman who asked was in riding pants, with a long jacket. Mud splattered her high boots and the tails of her coat. Her hair was neatly tied in a series of tight braids that bounced against her neck, enhancing her deeper complexion.

Kan'sa nodded. "Yes, we saw him leave moments ago." She pointed down the hill.

"Thank the Speaker," the woman replied, letting out a breath. "Sneaky bastards came in while I was out." She rolled her tongue in her cheek, before murmuring softly, "Adam better be grateful I breed the best when he's back."

"I take it you're Hawkfel's stablemaster," Kan'sa pressed as the woman crossed her arms.

"Well, look at you, putting two and two together like that," the woman answered. "You're pretty funny looking for an elf, you know? Not that elves aren't already funny looking."

"I'm a Hantheer."

The woman whistled. "So, you're the one folks are talking about, huh? Good to know. Claire would probably like to meet you then." She looked down at Diana. "And who are you? Some lucky dwarf who got to tag along on a quest around the world?"

"I'll call it lucky when we actually figure out what she's looking for," Diana replied, not backing down from the woman's retort. "Right now, though, I'd be happy just to have a real bed again."

"Ha, I like you, dwarf!" The woman laughed, grinning back at Diana. She extended her hand. "Eveningstorm. Emelie Eveningstorm. Like your friend spotted, I'm Lord Frederick's stablemaster, horsemaster, beastmaster, whatever the pricks in pants what to call it. I deal with the animals—

that's usually the men who get drunk off their asses at the Pleasure."

"Diana," the dwarf answered, returning the handshake. "This is Kan'sa, the savior."

"We were looking for your oratory," Kan'sa added. "Wondering if they could help me interpret the Speaker's Will."

"If you want to speak to a cleric, the oratory is right back there," Emelie explained, tipping her head back to point toward a white-walled building. It had the same rugged frame as most of the buildings in Hawkfel, but the stained-glass windows and clean exterior made it stand out against the mud-plastered buildings neighboring it. "But you might want to take a bit walking in there. Mother Helena has been looking for a sign to push Hawkfel to fight for a while now, and she might take to you for that sign," Emilie laughed, turning away for a moment. Again, she lowered her voice, "Ah, suppose Claire will get onto me for that one." Shrugging, she gave Diana another look up and down. "Y'all are decent enough looking folk, so let's trust the Speaker really did send you and you don't need to be tricked into nothing. Suppose it's no secret now that Hawkfel is the heart of the rebellion in Daendra."

Diana's brows furrowed. "And you'd just say it like that, out flat? Are you serious?"

"I'm as serious as the Speaker's Will! Don't tell me the dwarves support King Arvon, because I wanted to like you," Emilie jested, a note of seriousness in her voice. Her brows bent into a deep V. "You don't, do you?"

"Hardly, but a single lord doesn't believe he can take down an entire throne, does he? Or that a sign would appear just for his cause?"

"King Arvon did it. And who said it was a single lord? Besides, here you are."

That rider was a messenger, Diana thought. But surely it would have been more obvious that the country was going to rebel soon. There was talk of it all over the roads. Everyone hated the family in power. Still, Diana couldn't drop her scowl. She knew there was tension, but to actually walk into town when a coup was being planned seemed like more than a coincidence. But she resented the idea of calling it a sign. Kan'sa was silent.

Kan'sa stated, "We are only here for

simple guidance. I can make no promises we will be staying."

"'Course," Emilie answered, the bitterness gone. "I'm sure the good Mother will be happy to get you on your way. And if you need any help getting away faster, come talk to me about what kind of deals I can make for the World Walker." Emilie half-saluted and walked off.

"Well, she was…" Kan'sa's eyes followed the woman for a while longer as she decided on the word, "spirited," before turning back to Diana.

"She's certainly better than anyone I've met in Dane," Diana replied. "Must be something about the air there that puts people off."

"I didn't notice anything," Kan'sa replied. Diana started to explain, but the slight smile on the taller woman's face said more than enough.

Shaking her head, Diana replied, "Come on, savior, we've got to take you to see a priest."

Dwarven oratories were small. Religious buildings weren't practical businesses, so there weren't many built, and the ones that were took up the least amount of space possible, with only minor exceptions. A human oratory, on the other hand, was an art museum. Beautiful. Stained glass lined the entrance, each depicting one of the founding priests or priestesses of the Spoken Truth. Unlike a dwarven oratory, though, these featured antlers far more prominently. Still, there was a visible lack of Hantheer, of the first World Walker.

As they walked through the entrance, Diana asked, "Are any of these people familiar?"

"Well, I've never met any of them, but they are all important founders of the High Seat," Kan'sa answered. "It was a World Walker who assisted them in their endeavor." She was silent for a moment, and after a bit, Diana realized Kan'sa was counting. Finally, she spoke again. "They say nineteen is a sacred number. There are eighteen stains here."

"Where do you suppose nineteenth is?"

Kan'sa pointed down the hall into the main chamber of the oratory. A few priests ambled about in the room, moving out of the way as if they sensed Kan'sa's pointing finger. Diana followed the gesture and found herself looking at a huge statue of a stag and tall woman. Kan'sa stated, "The first Blessed."

Still not a World Walker, but the stag was blatantly modeled off a hart. Of course, it was too small to be called a hart. Kil'thian would have been insulted. Diana blinked, realizing Kan'sa had kept walking, heading toward the statue. "Hey, I knew that! Who else would they put in the center of their oratory, a Requite god?"

"I pray you are only joking, child," a cleric snapped as he passed them. Diana drew her nose up.

"Why not a Hantheer?" Diana asked, lowering her volume to avoid the attention of uptight clergy.

"It is an interesting question," Kan'sa replied. "There is a story about the first World Walker, I know. Allow me some time to recall it and perhaps we'll find your answer."

"Is any of this similar to your oratories?" Diana asked, bringing up their conversation from earlier.

Kan'sa pressed her lips together, studying the panels for a moment. "No, but this is a very

interesting design. There is a reverence for the wilderness that I believe only Daendrans could capture."

"This building was constructed by dwarves, I assure you," a cleric replied, approaching them. She wore a grander cloak than the others, marking her higher rank, a Mother.

Diana laughed, trying to make the noise less obvious but failing. "No, it's definitely Daendran-made, like the fort. Daendran through and through." The Mother started to reply, but Diana cut her off, "I think I would know dwarven architecture if I saw it, Mother."

The Mother blinked, and then it suddenly dawned on her. "Oh! Forgive me, I didn't realize. I have never seen a dwarf in Hawkfel. I mistook you for a child, my—" She paused for a moment, catching herself from adding the traditional "child" to the end of the sentence. She nodded instead, a brief "hm" in place of the phrase.

Good to know the oratory is being honest, Diana thought, not surprised that they hadn't seen a dwarf if they're lying about who built their fortress. Diana nodded. "Glad my face looks that young."

"In truth, it was more your...

children, what may I help you with today?" the Mother inquired, giving up on defending herself.

"Mother Helena, I presume?" Kan'sa pressed. The Mother, grateful for the change in topic, turned to Kan'sa. "I wish to ask for some interpretation on my quest from one so close to the Speaker while they cannot answer me."

"Surely, what quest has the Speaker sent you on?"

Diana and Kan'sa exchanged a look. How oblivious was this woman? With a slight twitch of her ears, Kan'sa bowed slightly, stating formally, "Well, Mother Helena, I am Kan'sa of Fahla'surni, World Walker to this age of mortality, chosen by the Speaker so that I might guide this world into a new era of peace."

Mother Helena was still, as if her mind was having trouble following. Finally, realization came to her. "Speaker's Will! He really sent you! You've come to overthrow King Arvon!"

"Oh, the oratory lady swore," Diana pointed out, nudging Kan'sa with her shoulder. "Does that make it all right for me?"

"No," Kan'sa corrected before picking up on Diana's mocking tone.

"Forgive me, children, I am overcome with joy," Mother Helena replied, her face flushed red. Her shoulders sagged in relief before she brushed her hair back into a smooth mass. "Hanmark has never been able to decide whether to support the new ruling family of Daendra, but I've known my whole life. On the part of Hawkfel, we ask absolution from our inaction and are readied to aid in this trying task." The woman bowed to them, before turning toward the altar and praying for several minutes.

"That's a bit dramatic, don't you think?" Diana whispered as they waited. "Didn't think Daendra let the clergy be so involved in its politics."

"It is unwise to mock one's devotion. However," Kan'sa paused, looking at the kneeling Mother before she returned quietly. "I know little of

Daendran politics at present. Perhaps this lord though doesn't believe in the separation of faith and government."

"Speaker bless you, Kan'sa

Fah'su'nina of the Hantheer," the Mother exclaimed as she stood up from her prayers, taking Kan'sa's hand and clasping it tightly.

Diana grinned. "Where are you from again?"

Kan'sa gave Diana a scolding sideways glance, but she saw the humor at least. "Thank you, Mother. And this is my companion, Diana Silverworth."

"Silverwell, you little—" Diana stopped herself, realizing Kan'sa was joking. Diana grinned and returned the look Kan'sa had sent her. She bit her lip, nodding as she gave Kan'sa a look at that read "Fair." She turned to Mother Helena, offering, "Mother, you might want to try again on the speaker of the Speaker's name before you go announcing her to anyone."

"A pleasure to meet you both,"

Mother Helena said, finally letting go of Kan'sa's hand. "Pray, what other guidance can I give you? Your task seems clear. Head for Vinhir! The people of Daendra need you to find a proper ruler for this kingdom, and the lord of Hawkfel is prepared to assist you if you provide him a path to follow forward."

"A rebellion has far more consequences than that, Mother," Kan'sa replied. "Surely you're concerned about a potential war."

"Would there even be one? Divinity has sent you, meaning that only the Requite Family would deny your actions," Mother Helena stated. "Kalmaran is civil though. They would not ignore the Will of the Speaker."

Diana turned and looked at the door. Enthusiastic stablemasters were one thing,

an oratory unconcerned about war was
another. "I don't think you'll get anything
out of her. She's putting her country over
her faith at this point."

Kan'sa sighed. "Thank you, Mother,
I will do my best. Since I know little about
the king at present, is there anywhere I
could go to research this noble calling
before I act on it?"

"I believe Court Advisor
Eveningstorm would know about that," the
Mother replied, smiling. Diana looked over
her shoulder, meeting Kan'sa's gaze.

Diana mouthed "Eveningstorm?"
Kan'sa shrugged.

As the two made their exchange,
Mother Helena continued, "You could find
her in the fortress, I'm sure. I will send
someone along to arrange an appointment

for you to meet this evening, during the lord's feast. He will be pleased to see you, I'm certain, as reminders of his duty. Until then, the oratory will provide you a room at the High Hawk. Anything to hasten your quest and provide you rest until you can ride for the glory of the Speaker, children."

With that, the Mother walked off to send out her orders. Diana and Kan'sa walked further into the oratory for a bit, studying the panels around the building. Kan'sa paid her respects to the central altar of the oratory. Diana said a silent prayer herself.

A few people trickled into the oratory as Kan'sa was praying. Diana watched them enter, eyeing Kan'sa with wonder. When Kan'sa finally finished, Diana jerked her head toward the small crowd, smirking. "You normally pull this much attention?"

Kan'sa smiled softly back. "No, but I suppose I will be."

Diana quirked a brow, looking back at the crowd. "There's something to get used to."

CHAPTER 3
THE PARTICULARLY CONFUSING TWINS & THE LORD OF HAWKFEL

Something between a crowd and mob was waiting outside the oratory when Diana and Kan'sa finally left. One of the younger sisters told the two they were invited to join Lord Hawkfel for dinner that evening, which began in the next hour.

"Sounds more like a command than an invitation," Diana said, straightening her tunic.

"If this man is gambling for a war, then I would hope he has at least thought this through," Kan'sa replied. "I am eager to see if he is a politician or a war general."

What's the difference? "It's not like he could be worse than King Arvon, not to Daendra, at least."

"I pray you are right, if this is the Speaker's Will. I won't have to live with the consequences as you will, not in the same way."

Diana started to ask but remembered Kan'sa had to leave once her task was complete. Part of her hoped that this wasn't Kan'sa's quest. She had only known the Hantheer for a short while, but Diana enjoyed her companionship. Or at least, she found traveling with Kan'sa better than living in Dane. And stopping in Hawkfel felt too brief of an adventure.

Kan'sa smiled softly as they approached the fort. "I'd rather it was genuine too. My people have known too many war hungry rulers looking for justification from the heavens. I'd hope my quest would begin a little lighter in tone."

The guards came to attention as the pair entered the fortress. Alert, but they took no action. Diana watched them nervously, having a fleeting thought of walking into a prison and a memory of other well-guarded buildings she had been in. She pushed the thought away; those memories tended to ruin parties.

Hawkfel's fortress had been built in a square, of sorts. The front was a narrow hall, big enough for two lines of soldiers pressed tightly together in rank. The left and right wings were filled with the workers, currently bustling about to fill the needs of visiting dignitaries. Diana could make out the fine drapery on the upper balcony of the back wall, guessing that floor served mostly for bedrooms. A few nobles leaned on the railing and watched the gathering, sipping on sparkling drinks.

They passed through the center of the fort, a garden courtyard, though it had a training yard feel. There was shrubbery planted throughout, but there was no color, no exotic flowers lining the way. It seemed like the space had been converted for the formality of nobles, less for an interest in gardening by the resident family.

Two guards pushed the tall oak doors open for them into the grand hall at the other end of the courtyard. Dark wood logs supported the room, with no shortage of antler decorations hung from the supports. If it hadn't been for the cold, stone walls around it, Diana would have thought this was a log cabin. The hall within seemed to serve two purposes. On ordinary days, it was likely for hearings and general counsel. For evenings and important occasions, it was a banquet hall. Regardless of its present function, Diana was positive that the wooden throne at the head of the room never moved. Whether it was business or pleasure, the lord's presence was surely always felt here.

"Presenting Kan'sa of Fahla'surni, World Walker, and her companion, Diana Silverwell," someone bellowed behind them. A woman's voice. Diana resisted the urge to look back to the announcer. The speaker's voice held a hint of a Kalmaranian accent, so odd in a place rebelling against a Kalmaranian noble. But turning would be rude. So Diana forced her eyes forward on the lord seated in front of her.

"Good evening, speaker of the Speaker, World Walker, and bearer of many names," the lord welcomed from his throne. His voice was steady, heavy, but warm. He was a soldier, for certain, but not cruel. He commanded the room like a lord, but he didn't command the people to watch. They choose to do so willingly.

"Good evening, Lord Hawkfel," Kan'sa replied. "Thank you for your invitation. We are honored to be guests in your house."

"And I to have you. Two races who

have never walked these halls, both on the same day under the same reign," the lord stated. "A good sign, I believe." A toast went up around the room, cheers for the oratory and its Mother rounding the tables.

"So your Mother would have you believe." Kan'sa nodded her head to someone in the crowd. Diana spotted the clueless Mother Helena smiling idly at the exchange. "May I inquire though what kinds of stories have been spreading about me since I have come to your city?"

The lord laughed, followed by much softer laughter echoed by the other members in the hall. Lord Hawkfel nodded. "Hopeful ones, I would say. I have been asked to lead the Will of the People, as you carry the Will of the Speaker. If I may be bold, I would see that those stand under the same banner." He paused, taking a sip from his cup. "Though I cannot say I would love to see war in my home, I cannot deny we are tired of King Arvon's reign over Daendra. It has been a long century for my people, for our way of life."

There were somber cries of agreement. The clergy bowed their heads, praying. Mother Helena was none too silent in her prayers. A few nobles toasted, taking slow sips as Diana and Kan'sa stood at the end of the hall, almost on trial. Diana clasped her hands behind her back, watching Kan'sa as the Hantheer thought.

"Tell me, lord, what claim do you want from such a campaign? And at what cost will you chase it?" Kan'sa asked. "The Hantheer believe in peace, which is why we intervene in your world through the

Speaker's name. To ask us to aid in a war is a very serious request. It must be for a truly noble cause with a truly noble goal for me to agree to stand behind your banner."

The lord teased his beard and eased back on his wooden throne. "I understand your concerns. You fear to aid a tyrant in taking the throne from another tyrant, which would keep things as they are."

"Precisely."

"I can promise you, speaker of the Speaker, that my goals are to save Daendra from people who do not know it," the lord said. "We do not want a Kalmaranian nobleman ruling a country that we founded and fought to regain from the Requite Family and its Requitidium. Daendra should be governed by Daendrans, by our culture, our customs, our people, not by royals from foreign lands."

Another round of cheers, "To Lord Frederick!" "To Lord Hawkfel!" "Daendrans serve Daendrans!"

Lord Frederick raised a hand. The room quieted as the lord rose, drawing his sword. "But I do not take on this task to unseat the king only to take the crown for myself. I will not falsely rally the hopes of my people." He turned the hilt toward Kan'sa. "I swear to you: I will not take the throne lest there is no other choice for our country. My quarrel is not a quest for a power, but to take the yoke of foreign powers off Daendra. Should I break this vow, you may take my blade and try me as a mortal, and I will not fight your judgment. This I swear on the Speaker, on his Will, and on my honor."

There was an intense silence in the room. It was a very serious thing to pledge on the Speaker's name, for the religious and for the less so. Diana wouldn't do so lightly. For a lord to say something like that, in front of his whole court and company was confessing treason, among other things. Diana felt her chest tightening, and the drinks on the table began to look far more pleasing.

"I am honored by your dedication, but can I question you further, lord?" Kan'sa asked, her eyes never breaking from the lord's. Diana was impressed. She would have broken under that kind of pressure.

"By all means."

"Daendra being in the hands of a Kalmaranian nobleman would mean that there are civil alliances between the countries, which is a benefit for your lands. If those were to break, if the current king were to be dishonored, war could devastate not only your lands but the Pledgeshills between your borders, if both allied armies choose to take their stands," Kan'sa stated. "At least with what the Kalmaranians would consider respectable blood at the head of Daendra, they are content to respect whatever court and internal affairs you keep. Why is the crown itself so vital to your people's happiness?"

Lord Frederick lowered his sword, nodding slowly. Then he turned. Dodging the question. All eyes in his court were on him. Diana shifted uncomfortably. The lord noticed. "Diana, was it? What do you think of Daendra's state?"

Diana blanched and looked at Kan'sa

for aid. The Hantheer simply nodded. Diana swallowed, answering, "I'm not really in the business of politics, but war doesn't help anyone. Least of all travelers." Which she was now.

"No one here wishes for this to be a bloody affair," Lord Frederick replied, turning back to Kan'sa. "Your fears are fair. I have thought the same, held the fear war could bring to our country if I chose to push on this rebellion. And I have waited for a sign from my Speaker, one that could prove without any doubt my actions are just. Kan'sa, speaker of the Speaker, you are a sign of peace. If you would aid this rebellion, surely you can see that both these things can be realized; peace for my nation and peace for the world."

"And what of the present king?"

Kan'sa inquired.

"We would send him and his family back to his people, unharmed. We will present this matter at the Council of Lords in two months' time. I believe between my allies and our rallied efforts, we will convince King Arvon to step down without any conflict," Lord Frederick answered. "As I said, we wanted our land to be our own. I have the power to rally armies behind me, should the need arise, but I do not wish for this path. But to stand by idly now would make me unworthy of my title. I am honor bound to defend my homeland. And I would ask that you aid us, if you are willing."

"There are concerns I still wish for answers on." Kan'sa paused, her lips stretched thin as she thought. "On whatever path it takes me, I will do my best to serve your people as well, in the name of peace."

A cheer went up in the hall. Kan'sa let out a long breath, loud enough for Diana to hear. They had been here less than twenty minutes, and Diana was already exhausted. She smirked at her friend, glancing at Kan'sa to make sure she was all right. Kan'sa nodded but kept her eyes forward.

As the cheering went on, Diana just barely heard Kan'sa muttering to herself, "Genuine wants. Still lethal wants. Ah, Speaker guide me."

After several minutes of the crowd's roaring, Lord Frederick raised his hand for silence. The hall dimmed only enough for his voice to be heard, "I ask that you join us for our feast, in the name of Daendran hospitality. And when you are satisfied at my table, you are welcome to my court advisor, for any questions I don't have the answers to now." He gestured off to the side of the hall, where Diana spied a familiar face.

It was Emilie, her braids had been drawn up in a bun and she was washed and adorned. The riding clothes were gone, replaced by fine silks, though she was the only woman of the court to be in a long skirt instead of a dress, cutting off near her knees. Breeches covered her legs between the rim of her skirt and her ankle-high boots. She noticed Diana's stare, and inclined her head toward her and Kan'sa, her expression purely neutral.

Diana grimaced and turned away. Did Lord Hawkfel not know his stablemaster and his court advisor were the same person or had the court advisor just lied about who she was when they met earlier? Before they could get any answers though, they had to eat. That certainly wasn't a bad addition to the evening.

To be perfectly fair, anything after the meal at the Hunter's Pleasure would have been amazing. It just happened that this meal was amazing on its own. There were four courses, each topping the last by a slim margin. By the end, Diana couldn't remember which dish had been best. Creamed potato soup, followed by cuts from a massive boar (which someone whispered the lord had killed himself), then venison custard, finished with fruit and cheese. All of this was accompanied by drink. Most of the court drank wine, but a few of the guards, and the lord, broke into a cask of dwarven beer. Diana took a stein for herself with every course. While the guards could only stomach a single mug with their third course, Lord Frederick downed two over the whole meal.

As Diana put away her fourth, ignoring the awed advisors around her, she nodded to the lord as he finished his second. He nodded back, a subtle sign of respect. Any human who could take that much beer must have a serious constitution. The lord turned away, boasting to the nobleman beside him. Diana made a guess why they would be speaking with Emilie instead of Lord Hawkfel this evening as he topped off his third drink.

"If you are still sober enough to discuss the state of affairs in Vinhir, I would be happy to reconvene in my quarters."

Diana turned around in her seat to

look at Emilie. The woman's expression was mostly blank, though she was eyeing Kan'sa with a small degree of concern.

Kan'sa hiccupped, then covered her mouth as she blushed. She laughed, "I may be a bit drunk, but I think it will clear."

"And you, Lady Silverwell?"

The dwarf chuckled, though her voice was steady, unlike Kan'sa's. "If you think that would make a dwarf even buzzed, you underestimate how much we drink. Or how much drink affects us."

The court advisor remained neutral, before shrugging. Her voice had changed since earlier today. She spoke through her nose more, with a hint of Kalmaranian in her otherwise Daendran accent. Odd, Diana thought. Like the announcer, perhaps even the same. Accents were easy enough to hide though.

Giddy and flushed was the extent of Kan'sa's intoxication. She grasped her head as they left the hall. "I believe I had—*hic*—a bit more than I should have."

"You weren't trying to keep up with me, were you?" Diana jested.

Kan'sa laughed, a loud easy laugh, before catching herself and saying much quieter. "Perhaps, but I suppose I should have known better than to try and keep up with a—" She managed to cover her mouth as she hiccupped again. "A dwarf."

Diana shook her head. "At least you're fun at parties."

The court advisor pushed open the doors to her office. The room was lined with bookshelves, filled with books with all kinds of bindings. Diana had no doubt the collection came from across the continent. A window framed the landscape of Hawkfel, giving a wonderful mountain view in the day, but now everything basked in cool moonlight and was hard to see as candlelight glinted against the window pane.

A huge, dark wood desk sat in the middle of the room. As the advisor took her seat behind it, Diana finally broke the silence, "Nice seeing you again, Emilie."

The woman looked at the door, and then back at Diana. After a moment, she smiled. "Oh, I see you met my sister."

"Sister?"

Extending her hand across the desk, the court advisor explained, "I am Claire Eveningstorm. You met Emilie, most likely this afternoon, I'm guessing, before Mother

Helena made us aware of your arrival."

Kan'sa gripped the back of one of the other chairs in the room. "Twins." The last letter dragged out a bit longer than it should have.

Claire nodded her head. "You are correct. Emilie and I are twins."

"Why are your accents so different?" Diana asked.

"We have chosen very different paths to walk. I attended college in Kalvari, while Emilie chose to work with animals here." Claire clasped her hands together and placed them on her desk. "You can see how we would end up very different people with such different careers in such different places."

That explains the accent, Diana thought. "What did you study in Kalvari?"

"Politics, mostly. Nasty business." Claire paused and let the silence hang longer than it should. "Lord Hawkfel is a rare type, as politicians go. More a soldier than anything, but smarter."

"What type is that?" Kan'sa suddenly interjected, and repeated, "I may be a touch drunk." She gripped her head, rubbing her temples.

"The rarest breed of politician," Claire answered, not missing a beat. "Lord Hawkfel is a good man."

"Rarer than dragons, that," Kan'sa commented, her cheeks still flushed.

"You were interested in discussing the state of affairs surrounding Vinhir, correct?" Claire looked between the two, not waiting for a response. "Where do we begin then?"

"A general summary would be nice," Diana replied.

"My people have no knowledge of this civil war—*hic*—that led to King Arvon taking the throne," Kan'sa added, her face tightly drawn, her words deliberately enunciated.

"Very well. Eighty years ago, a lesser noble from Astior held the throne of Daendra. In a matter of weeks, the Lilithin, King Arvon's family, came through Daendra and wiped out all Daendran noblemen and seated their own men as lords. They then proceeded to take the crown. In that eighty years, only one hundred of those nobles have regained their titles, and none of which have been in Vinhir."

"I gave roughly the same summary a week ago when Kan'sa turned up here,"

Diana stated. "There isn't anything more to the subject?"

"That is the issue. The entire war is heaped in mystery. The transition happened in a matter of days, and yet no one can explain how. Arvon had no army to speak of before, and suddenly he was the ruler of a foreign nation," Claire answered. "Anything beyond that is either the list of lords who were killed, or rumor and speculation."

"What would rumors say?" Kan'sa inquired.

"Some rumors would put the Cult of Reapers at the center of everything, but I suppose you would be interested in the less extreme." Claire stood up and walked over to her shelf. She pulled a journal off the shelf and returned to her seat. "There are some accounts from the staff of dark goings on and screams in the night, but nothing anyone saw. There's no evidence of this dark business. The would-be King Arvon was visiting from Kalmaran, and then, he was king.

"The records are from servants though, people who have either vanished or died, but still leave us with no evidence," Claire finished, opening the journal. She turned it to face Diana and Kan'sa. The pages were filled with scrawling from maids and gardeners and other staff members from across Vinhir.

Diana drifted off into the pages, skimming passages as Kan'sa and Claire talked.

"The visiting lord keeps to his chambers most days. I don't think he's actually spoken to King Ivan."

STOLEN SECRET

"There's something odd in the air lately. Makes me feel like I'm going to catch the bloody cough. I don't like it. It comes off that Kalmaran noble and his lot. Nothing but bad business, if you ask me. Of course, no one is."

"People have started going missing. This nice fellow from the armory was the first, then that pencil pusher that follows the Lord Arvon around. Slip of a man, wonder if he just blew away. Odd though. He seemed like a decent fellow."

"I've been sick since that lord showed up, like there's a weight in my head but no cold. Bad sort. Bad news. 'Course, wife doesn't believe me when I say it."

These kinds of comments repeated, revealing nothing, but all of them said the same thing. Lord Arvon brought darkness with him, people were going missing even before the killings started, and most of the people who noticed got sick. None of it sounded pleasant, but Claire was right. Anything could have caused that. A random plague in the castle, possibly brought by the foreigners, mistrust toward Kalmaran in general causing hostility, bad census that year. Odd, but not evidence.

Diana was pulled from the book suddenly as Kan'sa slammed her hands on the table. The Hantheer was leaning over the desk, her face flushed crimson. Diana wasn't surprised she hadn't noticed it against Kan'sa's skin, it was almost the same color. Kan'sa was livid as she leaned over, and Diana wondered what she had missed.

"I am not—*hic*—a charity!"

"I-I didn't mean to imply—"

"Y-you—*hic*—want..." Kan'sa staggered back, gripping her head. She shook it, stepping away from the desk, grabbing at the back of the chair. The motion wasn't wild, but it was directionless. "Want. Want. You all want me. I'm so—*hic*—wanted."

"My lady, what did I say?" Claire pleaded, standing up. "I beg your forgiveness."

Without answering, Kan'sa left the office. No polite nod. No dismissive wave. As the doors swung shut, Diana looked between the door and Claire. "What happened?"

Claire's face burned pink. "I asked her if I could serve as her ambassador after this matter is over with Lord Hawkfel. She didn't seem to take it well."

STOLEN SECRET

Diana pushed the journal back
across the table before she turned and raced
after Kan'sa. She pushed her way through
the remains of the party, racing through the
courtyard. She saw Kan'sa, a dark shape
stalking away toward the cliff. Diana rushed
to catch up with her.

"What was that about?"

"Nothing that concerns you," Kan'sa
growled, her control breaking.

Diana stopped and watched Kan'sa
walk ahead several paces. She shouted,
"What do you mean it doesn't concern me?
I'm traveling with you, aren't I? Having
someone out there spreading your quest is
good for us, isn't it?"

Kan'sa turned on her heel. Her
words were suddenly very sober. "You want
nothing to do with my quest any more than

the adventure, Diana. You will not follow me into its tragedy and hardships. You cannot. When this war happens, you will leave, or you will die. I will not lead Daendra or Claire or you to slaughter."

"War? I thought you didn't want to start a war," Diana prodded. Kan'sa roared and turned away. "What, now I'm bothering you?"

"It doesn't concern you, dwarf."

Diana gritted her teeth. "Is that all I am to you? Some midget tagalong?"

Kan'sa recoiled and, in her drunken stupor, she realized what she had said. Yet, she didn't take it back. "Don't do this."

"I was asking because I thought we were friends! I sold my apartment to come on this adventure with you! And gave you practically all the money to equip yourself! I gave up my business and security and normalcy to help you chase down these answers! I fucking killed that asshole for you on day two of this *quest*! And you think I can't protect myself? That I won't run into danger for you?"

"I didn't ask you to do that!" Kan'sa screamed, followed by a choking sob. "I didn't ask for anything, and yet you did—*hic*—it. Am I obligated to help you now because you showed me kindness? Am I to blame for your decisions?" The Hantheer stood taller, her head turned to hide what Diana could only guess was bleary eyes. "Or do you have no sense of—*hic*—responsibility in your own actions?"

"What the hell is wrong with you?" Diana had meant it as a roar, but it had come out as a whisper.

Kan'sa clenched her fists, balling them up tight. Diana's eyes widened. She hadn't seen Kan'sa fight, but she didn't need to know how long Kan'sa had trained to know that she didn't want to be on the receiving end of those fists. Despite her better judgment, Diana snarked, "What, are you going to beat me into silence?"

The Hantheer's knuckles turned white, but instead of saying anything, Kan'sa walked away. She stalked off down the slope away from the Hawkfel fort, a little stumble every few steps, and kept going until Diana couldn't spot her in the darkness.

Diana held her hands up and found herself shaking. What just happened? She let her breath out between her teeth, before turning and walking into the inn closest to the fort.

The innkeeper was curious where Kan'sa was, his tone too energetic for Diana. She almost barked at him, but she kept her anger tucked away. He didn't deserve to be shouted at any more than she did. Or Kan'sa did.

Eventually, he gave up trying to see the speaker of the Speaker, and gave Diana a room, courtesy of the oratory. Diana was glad to finally get away from everyone. The room had obviously been cleaned recently in honor of the noble Hantheer. Diana threw off her clothes and went into the private bath, not feeling guilty in the slightest about taking advantage of the luxury Kan'sa had stormed out on.

Week-old dirt was caked to Diana's skin from camping. She looked at her palm, at the grime beneath her nails and the dirt dried to the folds in her skin. The last bit of Dane was still there.

Diana scrubbed herself clean. She wasn't going back. Kan'sa or not, she had put that part in her life behind her. She could get a job as an enchanter. She was sure some capital would love to have a real dwarven enchanter locally instead of importing the service. She hadn't left Dane for Kan'sa.

Letting the filthy water drain out, Diana refilled the basin. She sat in the water until her skin pruned. It was a luxury she never had, and she wasn't going to waste it before she started a new life at the bottom. Again.

The warmth faded from the water, and Diana pulled herself out. She shivered as the air felt cold on her skin, quickly wrapped a towel around herself to dry off before crawling into the bed, still partially damp.

There was a down comforter and soft pillows. Most likely this was reserved for visiting nobles or lords who didn't stay in the fort's guest wing. Meant for a savior of worlds but given to her instead. She looked at the pile of clothes crumpled on the floor, filthy from the few days she had spent with Kan'sa. A friend, that's what she had called Kan'sa, but perhaps she should have withheld that label between them. It would have made this evening hurt less.

Diana tugged the comforter around her and curled up for warmth. She wished she had something nice to sleep in. She'd always slept naked in Dane, where her apartment was kept warm by the earth. Now she was above ground and cold. She felt exposed.

And small.

CHAPTER 4
SOMETIMES CRYING
HELPS

Diana climbed out of bed. She wished she had time to wash her clothes but, sooner or later, the innkeeper would start asking about Kan'sa, and with no Hantheer, Diana's window for luxury was going to run out soon. She pulled some slightly cleaner clothes out of her pack, threw in her clothes from the day before, got dressed, and walked out of the room.

Her guilt got the better of her as she walked into the entrance hall of the inn. The owner was away, so Diana left a stack of coins on the counter. As she walked out of the inn, she started counting how much coin she still had in her purse and whether that was going to last her until Vinhir. Her magic notes were heavy in her bag. Would it come down to food or her hobby? Thank the Speaker Kan'sa hadn't run off with the small pouch, but even it wouldn't last forever.

"Good morning."

Stopping in her tracks, Diana looked up at the familiar someone in front of her. Kan'sa's face was exhausted and tear stained. Diana stuffed her coins away and replied as calmly as she could, "Good morning."

"I'm going to Vinhir, if you need someone to travel with," Kan'sa stated, almost friendly. But there was still a tired edge in her voice. The tension between them was palpable. After a moment, Kan'sa looked away.

"As what? A companion or a bodyguard?" Diana asked, regretting it as soon as she said it.

"Diana, please," the Hantheer begged.

Diana swallowed hard. "Just call me stoneheart, it would make all of this easier."

That was low, Diana thought. She couldn't look Kan'sa in the eye either now. On her own, Diana started walking out of Hawkfel. Kan'sa followed quietly behind. The silence between them hung like a shroud.

Days passed. Kan'sa didn't call for Kil'thian. Diana asked once if he was all right. Kan'sa said he was, and they returned to their silence. It was going to be a long walk to Vinhir at this rate.

On the fifth day out of Hawkfel, Diana finally approached the subject. "What happened in Hawkfel?"

"I don't want to talk about Hawkfel."

"And I don't want to lose a friend."

That got Kan'sa's attention. The light of their evening fire shadowed different portions of her face, making it difficult for Diana to read what Kan'sa was thinking, but she knew that at least Kan'sa was thinking about something. And that was a start.

Diana straightened herself, fishing around the fire with a stick. "You were so mad about people wanting so much of you. And maybe it's pushing something sore, but right now, I just want an explanation."

"I am not a graceful drunk," Kan'sa admitted.

"Clearly."

There was a brief break from the tension. A slight chuckle at the comment before the heaviness returned. Diana turned back to her fire, expecting more silence.

"But that doesn't explain all of it." Kan'sa let her shoulders relax, defeated. "Diana, it's impossible, the expectations this world has on a World Walker. The Hantheer live long lives, longer than any mortal race. For my people, I am young and untested, yet burdened with a quest that's completion may be entirely ephemeral. Worse, when I finish, I will not know if I have succeeded until another calamity comes to this land, supposing I survive to see another World Walker survive their quest as well.

"In Hawkfel, the weight of that hit me," Kan'sa went on, her eyes fixed on the fire. It crackled, casting a dark shadow over Kan'sa, and Diana. "I have trained all my life to bear this weight, ever since I could stand on my own. I have been told every day that I would carry the fate of nations on my shoulders. But the true breadth of that, the real weight of my role, I could never have prepared for that reality. When Lord Hawkfel asked me to be his sign, to guide his people, when Claire asked me if she could spread my quest regardless of the odds, when you—souls put in my hands. Souls I know I must defend, but how can I live with the death of any one of them? I could start a war simply by siding one way or another. Thousands of those souls lost because I didn't have the foresight, the skill, or the time to make the right choice.

"And so, drunk, I broke. I let my fear guide me. My fear manifested in my words and I let myself believe them, despite the truth. I stumbled, but I thank the Speaker that they let it only be in Claire's chambers. The fear I could have caused," Kan'sa trailed off, shaking her head. "I have always tried to wear my mask, to hide my true self. My master told me it was to protect the people. If they saw me afraid, then they too would fear the world. I am a symbol of hope. I am salvation, sent from the Speaker. I cannot know fear. And I nearly let the mortals know I did. When you chased after me, when we fought, I didn't know what to do.

Nothing prepared me for what that pit would feel like, and my mind said things I would never say, would never feel, about you, Diana. Not in my right mind, not without the pressure of my task."

Diana let Kan'sa's words sink in. It was a lot more than she had ever considered in her life. The fate of the world wasn't anything she ever had to worry about beyond trade and whether she got out of range of one of her scrolls. To have the entire world on her shoulders was incomprehensible.

"I am sorry," Kan'sa went on. She let out a long-drawn breath. "You were right. You have already followed me into danger. I should not have let my fear tell me you would not continue to fight with me."

Still, Diana couldn't find the words.

She could feel them, pressing down on her tongue like lead, but they wouldn't come out. Kan'sa's ears folded back as she lowered her head, seeming to accept Diana's silence.

"I didn't leave Dane for you," Diana said, meekly, as if she wasn't even sure she was speaking. Kan'sa looked up across the fire. Diana shifted, fidgeting with her fingers around the stick. She knew that feeling, that pit. She had been drowning in it in Dane for years. "For whatever doubt you have, I left Dane because I was tired of being insignificant. Tired of being nothing more than a silver trinkets trader. When we met, you asked if I wanted to go on an adventure, talking about the sights you hoped to see, about the hope you wanted to bring to people. About making a difference. It was impractical to even consider just throwing my life away for that, but I needed it. I needed to leave Dane. And I needed a reason to leave. I have felt guilty every day since then, feeling like you were my excuse to leave it all behind. But you weren't. You were the-the-I don't know, the fucking kick in the ass I needed to get out the door. But I'm here now. And I'm not here because of you. I'm here because I want to be here. But as long as you're here too, I'm pretty ok with that."

Kan'sa lifted her head to look at Diana, an inquisitive expression in her eyes. Diana rocked her head to the side, weighing how deep she wanted to delve into her homeland. "There are laws underground, traditions that no one can break. I left the Kingdom for Dane because being in that country was breaking me for resisting it, molding me into everything it wanted from me and everything I hated about it. Another dwarf in the castes in the inescapable darkness. I was choking on the expectations everyone had of me. Dane wasn't all sunshine itself, but I was in Daendra. My...my past couldn't catch up. But Dane would have killed me too, if I stayed. Nothing could be worse. Dying on the inside like that. I'd prefer not to, but I'd rather go fighting with you than wither away underground."

The silence returned, but the resentment was gone. There was still something hurting there, but it could start healing. Something between the two of them, and something else in Diana. Something she hadn't thought would ever heal.

"I didn't mean to give you a full confession like that," Diana laughed, rubbing the back of her neck.

"It all needed to be said, even when it hurts. But we can do better."

Diana grinned, twisting her stick in the fire. "I could agree to that.

It was a start, at least. The tension relaxed between them as they kept traveling. Kil'thian rejoined them after another few days, which made traveling go quicker. Unlike when they were traveling to Hawkfel, Kan'sa and Diana spoke throughout the day instead of keeping to themselves. Diana found herself being more honest with Kan'sa and, in turn, Kan'sa dropped the mask she had been wearing when they were alone, voicing her fears when they surfaced. It wasn't easy, but it was better. And day by day, it got better.

It took another half week until they approached Vinhir. The city loomed in the distance with its huge white-grey stone walls. The castle was similar to Hawkfel's fortress, rugged but absolute. It was much larger though, towering at least twice as tall and three times as wide, with light glittering off the points of the towers in the daylight. The city stretched out around it, in a grid that petered out the farther it got from the castle; the quality of shops becoming poorer and poorer the further they were from the center. Still, everything remained connected and alive. Even in the outskirts, the roads were paved or cobbled to some degree. Having quality roads in farmlands certainly made Vinhir better connected. Diana wondered if the quality would ever leak over to Dane.

It was obvious to Diana why Vinhir had been built as a capital as they approached. While not as massive as the mountain ranges that ran through Daendra as a whole, three moderate peaks towered around the northern side of Vinhir, cupping the city in a mountain valley from behind. It made the location extremely defensible—even more so than Hawkfel. She wondered how Lord Frederick planned to circle a city that backed itself up against mountains.

About a day's ride from Vinhir, Kan'sa sent Kil'thian back into the woods. Diana appreciated that they wouldn't be making as grand an entrance as in Hawkfel, though she had gotten used to Kil'thian's steady pace and arrogant company. She wouldn't say it though because that would only bloat an ego that didn't need to be bloated.

"So, what are we going to do in Vinhir then?" Diana asked as they sat by their fire. Kan'sa wanted one more night outside the city, and so they hiked back up the road and camped a mile away from where the farmlands of Vinhir started. They found a glade among the evergreens in the one forest still left near the city, setting up camp about a mile off the main road. "Wait around until the good lord gets here?"

"Investigate, I would think," Kan'sa answered. "I want to know more about this rumor Claire spoke of. There would be a short list of mortals who would still be around from that time. Few remember anything that happened, so firsthand witnesses will be difficult to find."

"There may be a record in a library somewhere in the city," Diana suggested.

"That would most likely be a court record, and the throne would also try to hide all evidence of this rocky transition." Kan'sa sighed. "We would have to get into the castle, and the only way I see that happening would be for us to give away Lord Hawkfel's plans. It's the only information we have with any worth to the king without confusing where my loyalties lie."

"And we're supporting the rebellion?"

Nodding, Kan'sa replied, "Yes, I support Lord Hawkfel. Whether or not he makes a vie for power, his heart is in the right place. Daendra has had many rulers, though allowing the political unrest to continue will tear the country apart. Seating a Daendran-born ruler under the name of the Speaker should bring the kingdom at least some peace to allow it to develop more thoroughly. But to stop a war, we need to find proof that King Arvon is not worthy of his title."

Diana didn't argue it because she didn't know how. Politics were never her specialty. She cared about taxes and trade, but any more than that, it was beyond her interests. She did trust Kan'sa's judgment, and she did like the lord from the one evening they had shared, so she hoped Kan'sa's gut was right.

They sat in silence, considering their course of action. Diana pulled out her notes and parchment and began to transcribe a new scroll to fill the time. Kan'sa began pacing, thinking of and then critiquing plan after plan about where to start their search.

"It's not like any news would be kept either…" Kan'sa muttered, a track starting to form where she was walking.

"Kan'sa, you should sleep," Diana said, still scribbling out runes, though her hand was getting tired. "We'll know more when we actually get into the city. We don't even know what the inside of the city looks like."

"You're probably right."

"Besides, it's not like your pacing is going to produce a magical answer out of nowhere, so we should—"

"Say that again," Kan'sa interjected, turning on her heel.

Diana looked up over her notes. "It's not like your pacing—"

"No, no, the next part."

"Producing a magical answer?"

"Diana, you're a genius!" Kan'sa exclaimed, reaching over to grab Diana by her shoulders. Birds fluttered off in the setting sunlight at the outburst, disturbing the otherwise silent woods. "Producing magic!"

"You've lost me."

Letting go, Kan'sa walked toward their fire. "Diana, what happens when you cast a spell?"

"Hopefully a fireball appears."

"No, no, no, after that. After the spell and its magic has gone off?"

Diana shook her head and put down her notebook. "Kan'sa, can you explain this idea to me? It's late, and I've been sleeping on roots for a week now."

"The air is hot or scorched or touched, yes?"

Sighing, Diana played along. "Yes, one of those things happens."

"That's true of all magic, isn't it? It leaves a trace. Residue in mana expended from the spell. Which goes on to fuel manastones, yes?"

"Yes," Diana replied, "but what does any of that have to do with Vinhir and eighty-year-old rumors?"

"The civil war happened too quickly, unnaturally so," Kan'sa explained. "In the few reports you flipped through, you said the staff noted an uneasy feeling, something strange in the air. Magic. Powerful magic, whatever it was, but magic. How else could

King Arvon create and remove an army so quickly? It wasn't real to begin with, or it wasn't from Kalmaran or Daendra. It didn't have to be. A massively conjured army, or one teleported in, perhaps. A spell so large would have left anyone nearby feeling odd."

"That's a theory though," Diana returned. "It's speculation. We don't know what those people felt. And we can't ask them."

"Yes, but a provable theory," Kan'sa answered. "Mage guilds have been around for years. Their tasks include measuring the ambient magic, by decree of the High Seat, yes? To prevent magic from becoming sentient or being absorbed into a singular person. To preserve balance. Unless that law has been removed?"

"Not that I know of."

"Which means if we can enter the mages' guild in Vinhir, we can see if there was an abnormal spike in magic then. Supposing we could prove that, we would have a start to supporting that King Arvon's claim to the crown was illegitimate or, at the very least, support why his family is unworthy to rule."

Diana thought about it. She was still confused about the point, but she added, "And even if they managed to do that, we could find a merchant's guild who trades in manastones. There would have been an increase. But I still don't get why it matters what happened in the civil war."

"Why was there no World Walker?"

"It was a little civil war—"

"That upset the balance of the world. There should have been a World Walker,"

Kan'sa replied. "Mortals know of only a few World Walkers, but there are many more. You remember us for dragons and founding nations, but we come for many things. Small stones can bend a river. This war changed the course of that river, but for what? Why would the Speaker not send a World Walker unless arriving at the time would scare away a more serious threat?"

"You're suggesting something bigger is going on here?"

"I am speculating, like you said, and that is all. But I believe we need to find what truly happened eighty years ago in Vinhir," Kan'sa stated. "That search will begin tomorrow and must be over before Lord Hawkfel arrives."

"Why is that?"

"Because we need proof beyond the

Speaker sending me that this is the right course of action or Lord Hawkfel will start a war. And right now, we only have speculation and questions."

There was no point in trying to get any more out of Kan'sa. At best, she was tired and having trouble keeping facts straight and, at worst, just plain delirious. If Diana wanted to get any answers, she would have to wait until tomorrow.

Tomorrow came too quickly, of course. Kan'sa, eager to prove her theories, pulled Diana out of her bedroll before the sun had come up. Mist and dew still clung to everything around their campsite.

"We'll get in before a crowd appears," Kan'sa explained. "It will make navigating easier."

"I think navigating is always easy when you're that tall," Diana mumbled, packing her bedroll back up.

"Why's that?"

"Can't you see the whole world from up there?" Diana yawned, shouldering her bag.

Kan'sa laughed, louder than the morning wanted. The trees around them seemed to groan in protest, but it didn't stop the Hantheer's mood from growing more and more cheerful with each passing moment. Diana clapped her face and forced herself to be at least awake enough to eat.

Diana went through the last of their bread as they walked passed the farmhouses. They, unlike the city before them, were beginning to stir. Farmers crept out of their homes to collect eggs and milk before the sun crept into the sky as the duo meandered through. A few farmers looked up, curious about who was traveling so early in the morning. When the companions didn't appear to be merchants or trouble, the farmers would turn back to their work.

The more expensive the buildings around them, the quieter the streets became. A few bakers were starting their first batches, a few doctors opening their doors, but the city was quiet and it unnerved Diana. She had lived in silent tunnels, surrounded by stone, and yet here she could see the sky and felt trapped.

Eventually, the sun did rise. Vinhir rose with it. The sun cast the city in gold, sparkling on morning dew and polished stone. Kan'sa and Diana walked down the more affluent streets, looking for a mages' guild. The paths went from gravel to rough cobblestone to almost smooth slabs of stone. The streets were cleaner the closer they moved to the castle, and the smell carried less and less of the stench of livestock.

"Are you sure a mages' guild would be in the wealthier districts?" Diana asked, yawning widely as the effects of her early breakfast began wearing off. "They're a little easier going about mages in Daendra."

"If the High Seat must see to the management of a mages' guild, then it would be somewhere where traveling clerics would want to stay," Kan'sa answered. "Less taste of the people, and more of the clergy."

"Right," Diana muttered, distracted by the smell of smoked meat and bread wafting through the avenues. Her stomach responded. Diana pressed her hand to her stomach and kept walking. "I'm guessing we're not eating."

"Have you solved the issue of our financial difficulties?" Kan'sa inquired.

"No," Diana moaned almost as loud as her stomach.

"Then are you willing to sell your scrolls?"

Diana clutched the straps of her pack tightly. "Not just yet."

"Then we wait until I can hunt. We can ration what money we have for an inn on the outskirts, more likely a tavern, and I can hunt, but we aren't in a court, and we have nothing to sell." Kan'sa looked down at Diana, who was dreary and tired. Adding poor food for the next month and a half didn't make matters much better. Diana heard the Hantheer sigh, before saying, "I'll see what hides go for here. We won't have much need for it. I'm sure someone will be looking for tusks and antlers too. Perhaps one good meal before we're confined to the lower class."

"I believe the Speaker really did send you." Diana smiled, a half-asleep smile. Kan'sa shook her head and laughed lightly. Diana grinned a little wider. "So, a mages' guild."

CHAPTER 5
CITY LIFE

Diana rocked her head back, her stomach growling beneath her palm as she scratched through her pile of notes with her other hand. She hadn't eaten yet today, couldn't afford it at the moment. Not when paper was such a necessity.

Their good meal was certainly the last for a while. They had an early lunch at the Streetwise, the only seafood-inspired restaurant this deep into Daendra, Diana was sure. She was pleasantly surprised at what the Mysthalese chef could do with freshwater fish and inland game, though the coastal accents in the dishes were clearly from Mysthal. And for the next three weeks, she did her best to remember that meal from the upper districts of Vinhir.

On the other end of the spectrum was the tavern where she and Kan'sa ended up renting a room. The Thankful Barrel wasn't horrible, but Diana felt like she would take camping over this. The whole place stunk of the cattle farm behind them. Everything was watery, not just the food. Diana was sorely missing good dwarven beer. She would have even taken wine over the thin ale and onion-cooked everything. And the dampness of the building didn't help either. It left Diana missing the cleanliness of the inns near the Streetwise, and envying the apartments rented to members of the mages' guild.

The mages' guild was their first stop on the first day in Vinhir; an easy find with the friendly locals in the district. The issue was that they wouldn't let Kan'sa or Diana into the guild hall to look at the notes, the libraries inside only being for members. The mage on duty at the desk mistook Kan'sa's appearance for some shifting magic gone wrong and practically refused to look in Diana's direction. They weren't customers, but they obviously weren't mages, and therefore had no business in the guild unless they decided to join. The clerk's exact words had been "Unless the Speaker blesses you himself as a divine exception, I see no reason why you would need our archives, madam."

Fortunately, the following day, a far more considerate and peppier mage named Lorraine was at the desk. Diana explained she was an enchanter looking for work in Vinhir, which was only a small embellishment, and was hoping to join the guild. The mage suggested that instead of a traditional exam, Diana produce three unique spell scrolls to fit her "arcane disability." And that was where the trouble lay.

When Diana said she had a huge variety of fire spell scrolls, the mage laughed. Diana needed to make a new spell on a new subject matter entirely. She had the notes for a working lightning spell, though she wanted to test it again. But fire and lightning barely counted as two separate spells. To stand a chance of getting approved, she would need to tackle some other kind of magic.

Of course, that would cost money. The paper, the ink, the wax, the manastones, everything. Not to mention time, which was disappearing almost as quickly as their coin. Kan'sa was hunting every evening, with exceptional success compared to human hunters in the area. Still, between the expenses for the tavern, food, and Diana's enchanting supplies, they were hardly netting a profit. But dropping the tavern was not going to happen. If Diana was going to create a spell in a month and a half, she was not going to be sleeping on the ground. And while the Thankful Barrel was arguably only a small step up from the forest, it had a make-shift desk and a bed, and Diana knew when to take her lumps.

Fortunately, Kan'sa hunting meant they could find open locations to test out scrolls. Kil'thian would wait on the outskirts when Kan'sa came back to sell her kills, and then take Diana and Kan'sa out to some clearing the two had found the night prior. They kept moving from glade to glade. The last thing they needed now was to be told off by some guard that they couldn't be trying to blow up the forest. Or to get fined.

The pine trees made for good practice subjects for tuning the lightning spells. Clear openings to the sky meant it was easy to avoid hitting trees. And Diana's new experiments left the resilient trunks unimpressed.

Diana set her head down on the

nightstand she was using as a desk. She rolled her middle fingers over her temples. "How the hell am I going to do this?"

No one answered. She was used to that. Kan'sa was asleep, understandably exhausted. She was going to leave in an hour to eat in the tavern's dining room before leaving to hunt. Again. Diana offered to come help, but Kan'sa said Diana was working just as hard figuring out this scroll.

She wished she could agree. Diana felt like she was hitting a wall. She figured she would try for an ice spell. She had made notes on it before but never completed any research beyond the basic runes. Everything she had tested so far had been too unstable for Diana to trust giving to the mages' guild. They would kick her out as soon as someone used it, she was sure. The spell could retain a shape for seconds before rupturing into a series of sharp spears. If Diana had cast a spell like that herself, it would have punctured her instantly. Even lobbing the scroll barely gave her enough distance to keep away.

The fact of the matter was simple though; unless Diana could maintain control over the spell's shape, the scroll would never be approved.

Diana sat back up, twitching her pen as she reread the runes again. The answer was somewhere in there, she was sure. Some problem in the runes needed to be fixed, some line needed to be added to maintain the structure. But this was the hundredth time she had read her draft since their test this morning, and she was no closer to understanding why it was unstable.

Fireballs maintained their shape over their entire duration. What made ice so different?

Kan'sa yawned behind her, rolling over in the bed. "Any luck?" she asked, her voice heavy with sleep.

"No." Diana sighed. "Do you remember if that library in the merchants' district was public?"

"No, I can't say I recall," Kan'sa answered, letting out another yawn. Diana heard the bed creak as Kan'sa walked over to the nightstand. The Hantheer loomed over her, looking at the mess of notes. "I don't get how you read any of this."

"Something the savior doesn't know," Diana joked. Kan'sa shook her head, but Diana heard her laugh, even if it was just a breath of a laugh. "I could teach you. There's a grammar system. You have to—"

Diana cut herself off, swallowing the series of explanations. "This is mostly self-taught. Of course, being self-taught when you have enchanters living near you is a lot easier. The only enchanters here would charge me for looking at their windows."

"Why don't you try the library then?" Kan'sa poured water into the basin that served as a wash bin for themselves and their clothes. Diana heard the water splashing on Kan'sa face, minimizing the room's foul smell.

"What if it costs money though?"

"If it gets you into the mages' guild, then it's worth it. You do a few days' worth of scroll writing, find out where they keep their archives, and then we leave. That should produce the information we need. At this rate, Lord Hawkfel will be here for his

Council before you get anywhere."

"Why do we have to get this done by then again?"

Kan'sa emptied their water out the window and started drying her face. From behind the towel, Diana made out, "Beyond supporting Lord Hawkfel? Because I suspect that King Arvon's true actions will be washed out when the rebellion gets here."

"Washed out?"

"It will be a protection," Kan'sa explained, dropping the towel, "Whatever Arvon did, if we don't find it now, we won't find it after. He'll cover his tracks completely this time. If Frederick's rebellion wins, Arvon destroys the evidence and flees the country. If the rebellion fails, then he burns the evidence to prevent another uprising."

"And why can't we focus on his more recent actions as king to dethrone him?" Diana still wasn't entirely clear on what Kan'sa was hoping to find, or why she insisted on looking at the past, not the present.

"Diana, the Speaker sent me," Kan'sa replied. "There must be a reason I'm here, in Daendra, and not in Orimbela or Kalamaran or somewhere else. If it was because of the rebellion, then why not have me provide guidance to Lord Hawkfel his whole life? Why not have me come as a sign to him sooner? Why now, right before the people snap, with little understanding of what happened unless we were meant to find out?"

"You're sure about this?"

Kan'sa placed her hand over her

heart. "I feel this here. The Speaker guides me."

Diana exhaled hard. "So, let's go along with your theory. I still need another scroll. Let's say we get this in a week. It'll take a week to get the scrolls approved, according to the mage we spoke to, and then we'd give it a week before I could get into the archives. That means we'd be, at best, finding this information the day that Lord Frederick gets here, right before the Council."

No answer. Kan'sa walked away. Diana looked over her shoulder. "What is it?"

A stack of gold coins landed in front of her. Diana blinked. "Where did this come from?"

"We sold a few of his spires." Kan'sa

pulled her longbow over her shoulder. Diana heard the door creak as Kan'sa swung it open. "Make it count, Diana."

The door shut. Diana turned to look at the desk. For Kil'thian's antlers, Kan'sa could have gotten a lot more. Diana wished Kan'sa had taken her for the trade. She could have bartered— No, that wasn't the point. Even Kil'thian was sacrificing to get this quest moving onward. Kil'thian, who would throw her off from throwing up near him.

Diana shook her head. "Speaker, I'm not going to be shown up by an oversized deer." She shook off her notes, prayed that those dried, and shoved her notes into her pack. Grabbing the coins, she stuffed them into her overcoat pocket and made her way out the door.

STOLEN SECRET

Kan'sa had already left by the time Diana made it downstairs. Skipped eating. Dammit, dedicated savior, Diana thought, she's not going to starve herself for this damn mission.

It wasn't terribly late, though late enough that most businesses besides restaurants and taverns were closing up. A few shops remained open, but Diana felt a pit in her stomach as she saw bookshops locking their doors. A library isn't a bookstore though, Diana thought. Still, she picked up her pace. And said a prayer.

As she went further into the richer part of town, fewer and fewer lights appeared. It left the streets dark and empty, and Diana missed the late-night bustle of the poorer regions where taverns would be open until the early hours of the morning.

Here though, the only sound was her feet over the stone slab roads. She cast a glance over her shoulder more than once.

"Thank the Speaker," Diana heaved, feeling her chest tighten. A light was flickering over the entrance, but it was there. Bless that little candle, Diana thought.

The library was silent. Diana saw a plaque as she walked in: "Funded by the Vinhir Oratory." I guess that means they're open all hours like an oratory, Diana thought. Hoped. She found walking in a library familiar and lost her voice as she stepped toward the front desk.

The dirin man at the desk peered over, grumbling when he had to stand up to see Diana over the desk. The candlelight silhouetted his coarse, craggy structure, barky vines wrapping around hunks of granite into a humanoid shape. A gravely tone came from a collection of ivy making the man's mouth. "What do you want?"

Diana forced her face to stop before it twisted in frustration. The last thing she needed was to be kicked out of the library and have to go back to their room empty-handed. "Is the library open to the public?"

"As an oratory," the man answered, his voice gnarled and rugged, "but we require donations from anyone outside the clergy to stay open—particularly in the middle of the night."

The gold felt heavy in her pocket. She doubted the librarian was telling the truth, but she didn't want to give him a reason to call a constable. She didn't want to hand over all their money either. Better she returned with a little bit—enough to get Kan'sa something to eat—to be more useful than just a pathetic wanna-be-mage.

This isn't the time, Diana thought. She pushed three coins into the folds of her pocket, enough for one last set of supplies for tests. I will find my answers tonight, I will get Kan'sa a hot meal, and I will get us out of this damn city with our answers. She had to stretch to set the coins on the librarian's wide oak desk, but she refused to let her frustration show.

As soon as Diana produced the stack of coins, the librarian leaned back. He pulled the coins behind the counter, counting them without looking at her. "What are you looking for?" he asked at last.

What to say? If she said she was looking for magical research, she would have wasted her money. Everyone knew dwarves couldn't create mana, couldn't cast spells, and, therefore, didn't need to know about magic. But if she didn't say anything, she imagined the librarian would just as quickly call the constable.

"I wanted to know more about the Blesseds," Diana replied. Not untrue, if not at present, and usually kept in the back of the library. "The High Seat, in general. I'm trying to get to Hanmark." Kan'sa had mentioned needing to visit Hanmark. But she reminded herself after that this wasn't true and pocketed the excuse for later.

"Never heard of a dwarf being interested in the Spoken Truth."

Diana frowned. "And it's a pity. I was hoping to set an example." The librarian wasn't taking it. "Please, sir, I felt the

Speaker guide me here."

The coins slid off the counter. He huffed. "I leave in two hours. If the next desk worker doesn't show up on time, then you do too."

"Thank you, sir."

Diana walked by the counter, not making eye contact with the librarian. She didn't run, not that she wanted to. Instead, she slipped into the dusty wooden shelves, vanishing like a ghost among the tomes.

"Diana!"

The dwarf jumped, rocking back in her chair as she woke up. Ink smudged her wrists. She blinked, trying to remember where she was. Kan'sa loomed over her. "What have you been doing all night?"

Diana blinked again, looking at the

mess around her; ugly, rapid notes littered the desk next to her journal. The contrast in her handwriting was startling and, for a moment, she couldn't read the scribbles on the page.

"I was at the library," she muttered, stretching in her chair. "The librarian tried to kick me out when he left, but I hid for three hours taking notes from a rune book."

"What?"

"I copied most of the important parts, grammar rules mostly, about some other spells too, but mostly the ice ones, and then snuck out when his replacement showed up," Diana went on. She felt like this was fiction, but the feeling of dread she had felt when she was hiding came back and she recalled the hysterical shouting with ease. "After that, I came back here and tried to apply it to my runes, but I guess I fell asleep."

Kan'sa looked at the scribbles, and then back at Diana. "I suppose I wasn't expecting you to have a night adventure in the library."

"I wasn't either."

"Did you figure anything out?"

"I think I might have found out why the spells were unstable, but it will still require testing before I hand over a spell. But I doubt I'll need more than one or two tries now. I understand the principles of it, adding additional runes to ensure that the temperature in the spell stays the same and doesn't melt. That's what was causing the spikes—" Again, Diana stopped herself. She smiled briefly. "But one or two more tests and it should be ready."

"I wouldn't imagine handing over an untested spell," said Kan'sa as she sat down on the bed.

Diana yawned. "How'd I do?"

The Hantheer laughed and shook her head. "Exceptionally well, though I wasn't planning on judging you. Still, I suppose we should have thought of this sooner."

Diana shrugged. "We couldn't have afforded it sooner. The librarian stiffed me all the gold you gave me, even though it was an oratory-run building. And you've been too busy to get me in for free, ignoring the attention that would have drawn on us, so that's our lot for now."

"A pity, but I suppose what Vinhir's library does is its and the oratory's business," Kan'sa replied. "We don't have time to ponder the economics. You have a spell to write."

"I know," Diana answered, stretching again. She fished out that last coins from her pocket and tossed the pile to Kan'sa. The Hantheer looked down at it and then at Diana. Turning to her notes, Diana said, "Don't skip any more meals. I don't care what it means, you're not starving for this mission of yours."

The tests went swimmingly. With the runes Diana had studied, she understood a great deal about stabilizing magic, particularly ensuring structures maintained their integrity, as well as temperatures, something she needed to add to her fire spells now. She made a few notes about it to start a new fire and lightning scroll with the stabilizing concepts later, but right now she needed to focus on elements she hadn't already mastered. That would have been a waste of valuable parchment. Though now she was interested in testing an earth manipulation spell, or leaving the elemental discipline for something more interesting, like shifting or illusions.

Diana rubbed her arms as the ice scroll she made changed from a smooth, glittering orb into a smooth barrier, the spikes now reduced to fine points barely the size of her fingernails. Behind the wall, a tree groaned, now pressed with the weight of the block of ice. Wind whispered through the trees, and Diana shivered as the ice crumbled away. It was the second time they had tried out this scroll, and both had yielded positive results like this. The cold hung in the air, but that was the cost of success. Still, Diana felt frustrated, as if there was still something wrong.

"It's effective," Kan'sa stated. "A practical defense against an attacker, potentially dangerous if you had something to tip it over."

"I'd rather not think about how it could kill someone at the moment," Diana replied, shifting uncomfortably at the topic. Kan'sa was trying to help Diana with how she would pitch the spells to the mages' guild, but the electrocuted guard still lingered in her mind.

"I do not enjoy violence either, friend, but these people are expecting a rebellion," Kan'sa said, kindness in her voice, as well as sorrow. "At least you could protect a few innocents."

"Do you believe in war then?" Diana asked.

Kan'sa frowned but thought about the question before she replied, "I believe that we should preserve harmony in the world, and that we should do all we can to avoid violence. That said, sometimes you must wage war to protect the whole. It is why I have trained in martial combat. I pray I will never need to use it for more than self-defense, but if there is war, then I am prepared."

Diana sighed and looked at the shards of ice. She glanced at Kil'thian, who loomed beyond the glade. She could see the spikes missing from his antlers. She had so readily jumped to using a spell on the guards, and Kil'thian had just as readily obliged. To Diana, it was always a sort of joke, the idea of using her spells offensively, of killing someone, but to the hart, it had been serious. Over vain pride, no less. Now she felt like she had blood on her hands.

"Diana, do not let it keep you from moving forward," Kan'sa stated, putting a hand on Diana's shoulder. "You regret the death, which is admirable. Remember that always and let it guide your actions, but also remember you have as much right to live as they do. They would have killed you given the chance. You acted in self-defense, and in defense of me as well."

"Right."

"I have already said I hope it never gets easier, but do not burden yourself for defending your life," Kan'sa finished, squeezing Diana's shoulder lightly.

The words hung on Diana. Part of

her felt a little less weary. She couldn't control what her scrolls would be used for, but she hoped they would be used in that same self-defense she had meant them for. She swallowed the hurt for now, ignoring the pain so that she could work out her sales pitch for the mages' guild.

"Your scrolls will be fine," Kan'sa said, reading Diana's mind again. "I have seen those, as has Kil'thian. No one is expecting you to create a masterpiece, just proof of capability. Which you have in spades."

Kil'thian snorted from the edge of the glade, trotting off.

"That bad, Killy?"

The hart stomped and bugled at Diana before vanishing off into the woods.

Kan'sa sighed. "I would suggest not

agitating our fastest method of returning to Vinhir. He likes you too. Don't ruin that."

Diana laughed but nodded. "All right, I won't call him as many names, but he needs to get taken down a peg or he's going to float off with all that hot air in him."

Shaking her head, Kan'sa went to collect their supplies. Diana let out another snicker before she started gathering her notes. This had to work. She had done everything she could at this point, and she knew the bar for entry would be low, but this had to work. For Kan'sa, it had to go right.

Kil'thian didn't return to them until they had already hiked halfway back to Vinhir, leaving the woods behind for gravel and dirt roads again. At that point, it made little sense to ride the rest of the way, as they would leave him a half mile from the edge of the farmlands anyway. The sun began to set before they reached the edge of the city.

"I suppose I won't get much sleep," Kan'sa said as they walked down the streets toward the Thankful Barrel.

"You're not going hunting tonight," Diana stated. Kan'sa started to argue, but Diana cut her off, "I'm going to need you tomorrow. This is your plan. I can do the sales pitch, but you need to be there to see it through. And you won't be able to if you stay up all night hunting again."

"How do you plan to pay for our room then?"

Diana stopped and frowned. That was the painful reality of this, wasn't it?

Money. Kan'sa was pulling all the weight for their financial situation, and she would be until Diana got approved by the guild. If Diana got kicked out for snooping around the mages' libraries, it could be even longer.

Kan'sa pressed her lips together and said, "We can manage a night. You're right. I'd like to be there too."

"We could camp," Diana offered. "I'm not writing anymore—"

"But you are presenting," Kan'sa cut in. "You ought to be able to concentrate."

"After this, let's go to Hanmark," Diana suggested. "See if we can't get a few funds from the faithful."

Kan'sa laughed. "Yes, I think that would be a good idea." Diana started to chuckle, but her stomach cut her off as it growled. After a moment though, she and

Kan'sa laughed regardless. Kan'sa squeezed Diana's shoulders. "We'll be eating better soon."

CHAPTER 6
A REAL DWARVEN ENCHANTER

"Now remember, you are looking for the records of mana traces," Kan'sa repeated. "Find more about enchanting and scroll writing while you're there too. I'm sure it will prove useful."

"Thank you, Kan'sa," Diana replied, trying not to sound bitter. They had been rehashing plans since Diana's scrolls were accepted three days ago. Last night had been the worst: Kan'sa mulling over every detail; Diana gnawing her stomach to near sickness. Diana tried not to complain. She knew how serious it was. In less than a week, the Council of Lords would be meeting, and Diana had to find the records by then.

Kan'sa let out a deep breath. "You'll do great. Get easy work. I'll see you this evening." Kan'sa started to say something else but stopped. With one more supportive squeeze, Kan'sa headed back toward their room and hopefully to sleep.

Diana sighed, trying to get rid of the nerves weighing on her. She could do this. She had received glowing reviews of her work. Nothing went wrong with the scrolls. Nothing was going to go wrong. She wasn't going to lose the opportunity now.

Who am I trying to convince? Diana thought, shaking her head. Her nerves really were getting the best of her now.

The first step was always the hardest, she convinced herself. She could take one step, right? People walked by, turning their heads slightly toward the immovable dwarf in the middle of the street. At least it was early enough that she wasn't really in the way.

Vinhir was glowing in the morning. The middle-class districts looked like the height of wealth compared to the Thankful Barrel, suddenly filled with life, unlike the vacant streets Diana had rushed through only a week ago. Diana doubted they would be moving to one of these inns though. Even if they had the funds, they were traveling to

Hanmark soon and the rent there would be even steeper. But with a position in a mages' guild, Diana might be able to get supplies for her scrolls easier. Small consolations. A membership would mean universal employment too. They weren't going to hold her to an office unless she was training there.

Diana put one foot forward, slowly pulling herself closer and closer to the door of the guild hall. She gripped the door handle, suddenly terrified about what was waiting for her. She was going to be a mage. A real mage. Who would have imagined it, a dwarf being a mage? It seemed like the punch line to a joke.

The door whined as it opened. That ruled out any stealth options, sneaking in late like she had with the library. She would have to find the records while she was on the job. The guild closed in the evening, which would give her only a small window of time to search. From the smell of the guild, there was a cook for the employees. She hoped that counted her.

Slowly, Diana took in the entrance to the guild hall. She had been here before, twice now, but it seemed almost like a new place today. She expected a sense of belonging, searched for it as she looked out the great glass pane at the front of the building, but struggled to find it.

"Good morning!"

It was Lorraine, the same chirpy mage who had told Diana she could use scrolls for her application, and who had reviewed and accepted those scrolls the week before. Diana clutched her rune journal, wishing she had more time to clean her clothes before coming, but when all she had was a wash bin to clean her belongings, this would have to do. "Morning."

"It's Diana, correct?" the mage asked. Diana nodded. "Wonderful. Your scrolls were brilliant! Particularly after you said you were self-taught. They don't teach scroll writing in the Dwarf Kingdom?"

"They teach basic enchanting in schools, but that's only minor runes unless you follow the field further," Diana answered. "Scrolls have to be fully constructed sentences, which is advanced university training for the grammar." She caught herself. Of course, a mage would know that. She pushed on. "My family was only interested in seeing me carry on the silver business when I attended, so not my major."

"You're a merchant then?"

"Was. I had a small share of silver in Dane from my family's business, but after—" Diana swallowed, regretting going down this train of thought. "Well, my family and I haven't been on the best terms lately. I was happy to leave Kamedur, and happier to leave Dane."

The mage frowned. "I didn't mean to pry."

"No, I understand why you would ask," Diana replied, forcing herself to smile. "You probably want trustworthy people working here, and I'm about as much of an outsider as it gets. I'll do my best to answer any of your questions, if I can."

"Right. In any case, I'm Lorraine. I'm the head of the guild here in Vinhir, recently appointed too. I'm new with the interviews." The young woman beamed. "I was hoping you could write some scrolls for us to sell here. We would provide the parchment and ink, as well as any research materials you might need. Oh, and of course manastones, but those can be recharged locally." She gave Diana a little wink, and Diana pressed her lips in a smile to hide her cringe. "The pay should be enough to rent one of the apartments in the district for a good six months."

Diana clenched her fingers. "If we're going to be completely honest, I'm not sure how much longer I'll be in Vinhir. I don't want to just come and go, but my companion and I would like to stay on the move."

"A traveling mage! How exciting! I

would love to hear more about this companion too. What's she like?" Lorraine clapped, before flinching at something. Perhaps nervousness? Diana let the thought pass. "But I completely understand. You are certainly not bound to this guild hall unless you started conducting research or training. Your membership in the mages' guild is international, excluding Astior, of course. Can't imagine mages would be respected there, hm? As long as you can pay your fees, your membership will remain active. If you can't for some reason, say you're in Astior, then the fees will roll over until you pay off the previous month's until we haven't heard anything for a few months. Then the membership will terminate, but you can expect a collector come tax season for your residence."

Diana winced. Lorraine mimicked the expression as she laughed. "Don't worry, it's not too much. At least, not compared to what you can make on scroll writing or enchantments. We know research costs a lot. But we do still need something to keep the doors open."

"How do you keep up with all that though?" Diana asked, still unsure about the fee. If nothing else, it seemed like she didn't have to pay it unless she wanted to keep her membership active, so she could just leave it if Kan'sa and her own funds were needed elsewhere. Then again, having a mages' guild membership gave her credit for her scrolls. She needed to start contributing to her and Kan'sa's funds and forcing her membership might keep her focused.

"With magic, of course. And don't

worry about not being able to be affected by magic, we can find dwarves with this method still," Lorraine answered, then paused. "That sounded a little bit more terrifying than I meant it."

"Just a bit."

"The spell has to be consensual, so we couldn't use it on you without your permission," Lorraine stated. "The guild uses a magic sort of logbook, for both mages and customers, to make sure mages are paying their fees and customers aren't robbing our mages." Lorraine walked behind the front counter and produced a large ledger. "You write your name in here and it communicates with all the other mages' guilds' ledgers, so if you walk into the hall in, say Fendune, they would pull you up and tell you how much you owe, along with the date you owe it on and where you last paid."

"Sounds like you could use that to track me," Diana replied. She tried to not sound concerned. It wasn't a big deal, she hoped.

"In a sense, I suppose," Lorraine answered, "but the ledgers are the property of the guild, and we work for the High Seat. Only a Prophet or someone from the High Seat's clergy could demand access to that information. Or I suppose a World Walker."

Guess I can't piss off any holy warriors, Diana thought. She didn't know why the thought of this unnerved her. It wasn't even attached to her person, just a record of her bills. Well, if nothing else, she could just stop paying the fees eventually and not have to worry about it. She walked over to the counter and signed on the line that Lorraine pointed to. Maybe she would have some dwarvish luck and be immune to whatever spell made this book work.

Soul still intact, Diana followed Lorraine on a tour of the hall. The cook was for everyone, resident mages were provided an office while Diana would have to use a common space to work, and the archives were open at all hours.

With only days to search, Diana pondered over everything she had observed as she looked through the rows of books with Lorraine. She didn't know where to start with such a massive task, and it didn't feel right to ask. Maybe some of Kan'sa's paranoia over Arvon wiping this information away had her on edge. So, Diana started figuring out how she could ask without saying exactly what she was looking for.

As they started to leave the archives, Diana asked, "How far back do your records go here?"

Lorraine paused, looking through the books. "Well, we have some texts with originals that date back several centuries. But as far as local records, we have some historical pieces as far back as two centuries ago. What's the interest?"

"Historical."

"Ah, I see," Lorraine replied, smiling. "Well, we have a fine library in Vinhir as well, if you'd be interested in visiting it."

The two continued on their tour for another hour, until Lorraine left Diana at a workstation and left the enchanter to her own devices. Diana spent most of the rest of the day writing out as many scrolls as she could, hoping to recover some of the cost of living before she had to leave. She pushed herself through the runes until her stomach started making her misspell her scrolls.

Diana tried not to feel guilty at lunch as she sat down for a good meal before Kan'sa had a chance for one. She wished she could have shared the moment with Kan'sa. The Hantheer deserved it more than her. Feeling warmth in herself again didn't hurt though. Unfortunately, Lorraine didn't have anything to drink, but Diana wasn't going to complain.

Lorraine checked in on Diana often over the next few days, chatting about Diana's work. Chiefly, this was enchanting or scroll writing, since Diana was magically limited. Lorraine kept saying, "A real dwarven enchanter!" every now and then, like Diana was a trophy for the guild. Diana didn't comment on it. She just wanted to get through her work, so she could take another few minutes in the archives.

The other resident mages weren't as excited about Diana as their leader, but they kept to themselves. None of them used "stoneheart" around Diana, but she thought she heard it from one of the older mages when she was leaving on her second day. No one in Vinhir, not even Lorraine, considered Diana a mage though. She was an enchanter, and that was where it stuck.

When she got back home in the evenings for the first two days, Kan'sa grilled Diana on everything she had learned. Diana started smuggling meals out of the hall for the two of them, which made the questions a little more relaxed.

It was hard for Diana to say she enjoyed the work for the mages' guild, for the all of six days she was there. She could take as many notes as she wanted, and the free food was nice, but something about the work didn't sit well with her. Perhaps it was Lorraine's regular visits, and the extensive questions the woman asked. Still, Diana was bringing back more than enough in wages to cover her and Kan'sa's expenses, though they had been putting the majority of it into saving for their trip to Hanmark. Then again, with the Council of the Lords meeting in a day, it didn't really matter.

Diana closed her notebook and sat back in her seat, stretching her fingers out after hours of writing. She had been trying to write extra spells without sacrificing clarity in her scrolls. The last thing she needed was a scroll to backfire on someone. Still, if she got her quota done before lunch, she could spend more time in the archives without anyone asking why she wasn't being productive.

Unfortunately, so far, her searches hadn't been fruitful. The mages' guild's archive wasn't a library, but it was cluttered, and people took books without asking anyone else and put them back without any concern about where they had been. Already defaulting to unwanted by her "peers," Diana didn't try to bother anyone with asking about what texts someone had taken out of the hall.

However, mana-level records had disappeared entirely. Diana outright asked

Lorraine about it on her fourth day and the mage shrugged and inquired why Diana was curious. Mana didn't affect her. Diana played it off as random interest, saying "Historical interest" again, and walked off. The conversation still bothered her, and the lack of interest in that much information disappearing rubbed her the wrong way. Would the lords feel that way too even if she did find something? Would her evidence be dismissed?

Diana walked into the archives again. She was running out of time. What she thought was only going to take a day or two had now turned into six. The Council would be meeting tomorrow. Lord Hawkfel would start his rebellion tomorrow, with or without this information, but Kan'sa's lead would be gone forever.

Maybe King Arvon already came through, Diana thought, looking through the records once more. Still, nothing showed up.

"What are you looking for?"

Diana turned around to face Lorraine. She managed, "Just records—" Why was she so unnerved by this woman now? Why did Lorraine keep popping up whenever Diana seemed close to finding something?

"Still looking for information on mana levels?" Lorraine asked, as cheerful as always. "I don't know what good it will do you. We get manastones anyway, so you don't need to worry about mana."

An idea came to Diana, or an idea resurfaced. Manastones. If there was an increase in mana, then there would have been an increase in stones that absorbed that mana as well. It wasn't just raw energy they had to look for, they could find records of increased manastones being found in the area. They didn't even need to come to the mages' guild for that. Why hadn't she thought of it sooner? She had, though, and had forgotten it to pursue the guild out of excitement of being a mage instead of saving them so much wasted time. "That's the thing though. I want to make sure you get a good deal. Trader in me. If the levels of mana have changed, then there should be a ready access to manastones, but if the merchants' guild hasn't lowered the price—"

"Diana, don't worry about it."

The tone was final underneath the sweetness. Diana stopped herself from swallowing. Now she was definitely unnerved. Whether or not Lorraine and Diana were interested in this subject for the same reasons, Lorraine clearly had a reason to want to hide the fluctuation in mana levels. And as Diana started to push the papers she was looking at away, Lorraine's gait became like an animal stalking as she walked closer.

"I-I'm gonna head out," Diana said, trying to minimize her stutter. There were a thousand and one reasons a mage would want to hide a rise in mana levels: so they could take advantage of it exclusively; so they could research magic easily; so they could use more powerful spells. All those reasons suddenly clung to Lorraine. All her questions, and Diana now started to realize how deeply some of those had pried.

"Is something wrong?"

"No, just, I-my companion, she was feeling ill. We've been staying in a really nasty tavern on the outskirts," Diana replied, backing away slowly.

"You mentioned. The Thankful Barrel, yes? I hope she's all right. You should take her to see a healer. Maybe she has a special prayer for the Speaker too."

"Shit, Kan'sa," Diana swore. Kan'sa had to be all right. She had to be. Lorraine followed Diana, smiling pleasantly as she cooed, "Is something wrong? Is your friend *ok*?"

Lorraine was uncomfortably close. She reached out, taking Diana by the shoulder. Something cold pushed against Diana's skin under Lorraine's touch, fighting to break through the laws of nature. Lorraine began pushing Diana toward the front. "Let's go check on her."

Diana didn't push back. The shock through her shoulder had jolted her. How? It tingled on her skin, pushing to get in. Magic. A magic so powerful it could push at her arcane immunity to leave an effect. She followed Lorraine's instructions numbly, swearing in her head over and over again as they walked into the entrance of the hall.

The front window crashed in. Diana and Lorraine jumped at the sound, glass shattering over the floor in front of them, but when Diana heard the bugle, she jerked free of Lorraine's grasp. She shoved her notes and tools further into her bag, as well as any scrolls she could grab off the front desk. She was losing time, but at least she could defend herself if Lorraine decided to do something besides throw information she shouldn't know at Diana. But she wasn't going to lose her notes. With her belongings and ten scrolls, Diana dodged away from Lorraine, who was staggering toward the counter now. White lines, whiter than flesh, started to appear on her skin. Diana could have sworn her mouth started to twist in on itself, swallowing itself up.

"I'm not going to ask why you're here, but we need to get out. Now." Diana didn't care if Kil'thian was hurt about her barking orders. The hart must have understood the importance. He had, after all, run through a crowded midday Vinhir, nearly to the middle of the city.

Diana jumped up onto one of the shelves and then onto Kil'thian's back. The hart bugled again at the mages that came into the room before leaping out the window. Lorraine stumbled to the glass, grasping the broken frame of the window as the two raced toward the outskirts of town.

"I think Kan'sa is in danger." Diana wasn't going to waste time on the merchants' guild. Not yet. Not until she was sure Kan'sa was safe. She would be asleep, unaware of whatever threat may be coming for her. Diana wasn't even sure that there was one, but then again, Kil'thian had appeared out of nowhere. Something must have been wrong. Harts were signs from the Speaker after all.

Kil'thian didn't wait for Diana to even

bring up the option of the merchants' guild. He was making a run for the Thankful Barrel. The good thing about riding a hart is that the horns scare folks out of the way a lot faster than a charging horse's gallop. And even with a few missing, Kil'thian was not lacking with his huge rack spread out like an ebony bramble.

Diana didn't wait for Kil'thian to kneel when they reached the tavern. She swung over his side and pushed off, landing with her knees bent, but sore from the drop. She didn't let it stop her as she raced for the stairwell up to their room, fumbling for her key, and continuing to run as she dropped it.

"Kan'sa, get up!" The door swung in, splintering against its hinges slightly from Diana's kick. Diana bent her knee once for relief before rushing to the bed, shaking her friend awake.

The Hantheer rolled over in bed. "Diana? What are you do—"

"I don't know how, but Lorraine knows who you are. She threatened you, said you would need a healer, and then Kil'thian broke into the guild hall, and then—"

"Kil'thian did what?!" That woke her up.

"Kan'sa, we're in trouble here. We need to go. Lorraine is crazy, she went all—" Where to start with what had happened with Lorraine? Later. "I know where we can get information about the mana levels outside the mages' guild. We have hours to find whatever it is you need to find, and there's only one other lead I know of. Come on!" Diana pleaded.

The appearance of Kil'thian seemed to convince Kan'sa something was wrong. Based on the shouting downstairs, he was still outside. The two shoved their belongings into their packs and cleared out of the room. With all the commotion over the hart, Kan'sa and Diana made it out of the tavern without worrying about their last night's expenses.

Kan'sa vaulted onto the hart's back and reached her hand out to Diana. Not caring about how it would make her look, Diana took the hand and let Kan'sa yank her up onto the hart's back. She felt herself ragdolled through the air before landing with an unceremonious thud.

As Diana adjusted her pack, Kan'sa was scanning the roads. "Are you sure about Lorraine?"

"I—" Diana didn't have time to finish. Heat streaked overhead until a fireball collided with the top of the Thankful

Barrel. The building went up in flames in seconds, the fire leaping to the next roof over. A bell sounded off at a nearby town, but Diana barely twisted to look at the other rider. In the distance, she saw a sickly figure with Lorraine's silhouette. The white was burning away at her skin, charring everything around it. "Yeah, I think she has a problem with you."

"Where to?" Kan'sa asked as she took in the figure, as well, kicking Kil'thian forward.

"The merchants' guild hall," Diana answered, her eyes lingered on the front door of the building, praying everyone got out. "Northern end of the merchants' district."

"Very well, but first, that," Kan'sa stated. "We put that down."

Kil'thian had a score to settle as well as they raced toward Lorraine. He lowered his antlers, the left one catching the bulk of Lorraine's midsection as they passed, dragging her through the air. Something screamed, but as Diana watched, she couldn't find Lorraine's mouth.

With a flick of his head, Lorraine fell off. Kan'sa notched an arrow in a breath, the plume plunging into what was left of Lorraine's neck. The shape heaved and went still, eyes bare to the sky.

Diana didn't dare ask the nature of Kan'sa's mumbled prayer.

As they clambered down the stony roads, they missed, only two streets over, a procession of riders as the Lords of Daendra entered Vinhir. They didn't particularly care, since it left all the roads between the

Thankful Barrel and the merchants' district empty beyond rushing emergency mages to the fire. Kil'thian flew through the streets, leaping any remaining pedestrians too slow to move or a response wagon that got too close. Diana clung to his mane, praying to the Speaker she wouldn't fall.

Kan'sa wrapped her arm around Diana, pulling them both off Kil'thian's back as they reached the guild hall. As she set Diana down, Kan'sa asked, "How do you plan to get their records so quickly? We don't have the time to be approved here."

Diana hadn't done this in years. She had been under duress from her father to do it back then anyway, his little puppet. She didn't know if she had the nerve to do it now. Then she thought about the fire at the tavern, about the thing Lorraine had become, about the lords riding to the castle, about Kan'sa giving up everything to give Diana a way forward.

"Watch."

The door snapped back. A few merchants disgruntled about being stuck here instead of getting to see the procession jumped at the noise. "We're not op—"

"I don't give a damn," Diana roared, memories of her family biting in her mind. Her father would be pleased. Fuck him. She hated having to use this namedrop, but she didn't have time to negotiate. "I'm Diana Silver-fucking-well. If your boss hears you turned out the heir to the biggest silver company in the Dwarf Kingdom, he will personally hand all of you over to the closest Mysthalese assassin he can find. Now, I've got fucking business to do with you shits."

That got their attention. The young men stood up. "Y-yes, ma'am. What do you need, ma'am?"

"Your manastone records for the past ninety years, at least," Diana answered. The merchants looked between each other, confusion on their faces. Diana barked, "Did I fucking stutter, gentlemen?"

"No, ma'am!" They sprung to their feet, practically falling over each other to get to their records.

"Effective," Kan'sa said. Diana started to defend herself, but Kan'sa just nodded. "There is a time and a place. I'm still disappointed this is how you must act to get people's attention, but if it works, I can't complain."

Diana felt her stomach twist. "Thank you."

"You're an heir?"

"It's complicated."

"We have a moment now."

"I *was* an heir," Diana answered. "Formally, I still am. I have no interest in it, but my parents giving it to someone outside the family would be a show of weakness. Which either means that they'd have to adopt the next dwarf legend or watch their business die. That's the short version at least."

"No siblings?"

"None that are outside of prison or old enough. Give it twenty years though and my younger brother might take the title. We're not...we'll see what happens with him." A flash of pain crossed Diana's mind as she thought of her younger brother, worrying only for a moment before locking away the feelings she had for her family. Now was not the time.

Kan'sa fell silent. Diana appreciated the quiet.

The merchants returned moments later with an old ledger. They set it down on the counter and opened it before stepping back, away from Diana's glare. Diana stepped up to the counter and began flipping through the pages as fast as she could without tearing them.

"It seems there was a significant increase recently of manastones found here," Kan'sa commented. "All the values are going up the further we go back, suggesting there was a lack of supply here."

"Who are you?" One of the merchants ventured to ask, the question pointed at Kan'sa.

Kan'sa didn't look up from the page. "Her security."

Diana grinned briefly as the merchants backed farther away. Kan'sa didn't need curses to intimidate people. Granted, it might have been the fact she was just shy of seven feet tall and carrying a longbow over her shoulder.

"Here we are, eighty years ago," Diana stated, reaching the back of the ledger. She flipped a few pages back to the years prior to the war. "There was a ninety percent increase in manastones found in the area of the city after King Arvon took over the throne."

"Does it say where?" Kan'sa pressed.

"No," Diana answered, shaking her head. "Dammit!"

"Lady— Ms.— Ma'—"

"Spit it out already!" Diana snapped.

"Y-yes, there was a large deposit of manastones found along the banks near where the sewers deposit into the Vinheran, the main river to the northwest of the city. Or-or that's what my grandfather said. Said the river was flowing with magic. Traders kept it to themselves to keep from having to drop prices for a few years."

Diana and Kan'sa looked at each other. Diana began, "That would mean a massive spell—"

"—would have originated from under the city," Kan'sa finished.

Kan'sa gave a curt nod to the merchants. "Thank you."

Pointing to the younger merchant, Diana ordered, "You get a full write up of this and deliver it to Claire Eveningstorm in

Lord Hawkfel's company in the next hour. She will be here for the Council. You give her my name and say it's for her rumors. You got that?" The man nodded. "Good." As he began to scribble, Diana turned to Kan'sa, "Just in case. It's a start for them."

"Then we best find something more substantial," Kan'sa added, gesturing to the door.

Without another word, they left the guild hall, leaving the merchants to wonder what in the world had just happened. Even after the events of the following days, they would probably never understand what had occurred that evening. But the young man did as he was told.

CHAPTER 7
SOMEWHERE UNDER
THE CITY

"Shit, this place reeks!"

The smell of the tunnel was rancid, even in the short distance between the entrance and where they were waiting. Diana laughed though. "You should have included this on the list of expectations when we met."

They had circled the city twice before Diana spotted the entrance to the underground network, dodging questions from the watchmen outside the city as they searched. It was only a matter of time before someone caught up though and made them give straight answers.

This was the only sewer entrance that let out to the Vinheran the three could reach, and with already avoiding the watchmen's questions, Diana didn't think the city guard would be much help. If they had any hope of finding answers, it would be within this round tunnel. Somewhere in that darkness, something was waiting for them. Diana wished she had more confidence about what that something was. Midnight had slipped away. Dawn was coming quickly, and so was the fate of Daendra.

Kil'thian snorted behind them,

pressing against Kan'sa's back with his nose. Kan'sa smiled and stroked the hart's nose. Diana tried not to flinch as she looked at Kil'thian's blood-soaked antlers. "We'll be safe, friend."

Clearly, Kil'thian didn't like that response, but there wasn't anything he could do about it. There was no way he was going into the sewers. With his amount of pride, even Kan'sa wouldn't be able to drag him in. Besides, he needed to clean himself— something he'd been attempting in the river rushing behind them.

An old, unlit torch was mounted by the entrance. Kan'sa pulled it out of its resting place and wrapped a bit of cloth around its head. In moments, it was burning again. Kil'thian let out a soft cry as the two walked into the darkness of the tunnel.

The walls were squarer to match the gates set around the filters for the water. Water rushed through the central canal, with plenty of debris floating with it. Particles of the current splattered up on the walls, making the walk slippery at best, squishy at worse. Neither gave Diana much comfort, and she scrunched up her nose at the sight. Despite being closer to it, the scent didn't get much fouler. That isn't to say it wasn't already unbearable.

"You'd think someone would be down here," Diana said as they passed the third open gate. The tunnel had yet to branch off into any other passages, connecting to other points in the city to collect sewage. Either they were walking over the beds of manastone now or they hadn't gone as far as they thought into the tunnels. Diana wished she could tell, but there were no markers to keep her bearings. There was no real change at all besides the occasional open gate. "With as big a city as Vinhir, you'd think they would have better maintenance for their sewers."

"Perhaps this section is avoided, or there are other, more recent channels," Kan'sa suggested. Rust corroded the gates they had passed through, and the torches had rotted away long ago. "This seems like the oldest part of the sewers."

"Which means it would need more maintenance," Diana replied as she watched the filth roll through the center of the tunnel. Most of it would get caked onto the tunnel's walls or be broken up enough that it wouldn't matter once it reached the Vinheran, but she would never look at the river water the same again.

The tunnel kept going, the same square path, with no signs of change for a long while. Then, the walls grew straighter, with sharper cuts. The stone changed to a darker material. What troubled Diana more was not knowing how long they had been in there. Underground, she had always been able to keep a good head for time, but here, she was lost. Maybe it was because it was mortal-made, unlike a true tunnel that was carved out of the earth by wind and water. This one was built. But by whom?

Other than the flow of water and their own footsteps, this place was silent. It was unnerving. Diana had never been alone in a mine. There were other miners there. Or if there weren't, she could hear the earth breathing through the tunnels. The air was stagnant here.

"Does it feel like a tomb in here to you?" Diana asked.

"I'm glad I'm not alone on that."

The torch flickered as they laughed. A gust of stale air came from in front of them, tugging forward into a current by some larger space. Kan'sa and Diana fell silent, looking ahead. Diana forced a chuckle. "I guess there's something close by."

Slowly, they walked on. Something thundered in the distance, masking their footfalls as they left the tunnel for a larger room ahead. And yet, there was stillness amid the din, now so loud Diana would have to raise her voice for Kan'sa to hear her. She watched Kan'sa's ears swiveling regularly, flicking toward every sound.

Suddenly, the walls fell away. In the same breath, the torch puffed out. Diana blinked a few times, her eyes quickly becoming accustomed to the dark. She gripped Kan'sa's hand as the Hantheer started to walk toward the middle of the tunnel. She called loudly, "Can you see?"

"No."

"Hang on then," Diana said, not liking how her voice disturbed the room ahead of them. "Hold on to that torch though."

Kan'sa gripped the wood so tightly it creaked. She loosened her fingers, letting Diana guide them through the darkness. Diana searched the walls. The chamber they now stood in stretched twenty feet to each side away from where they stood. There was a bridge in front of them where the canals merged into the one they had followed in. They crossed it, water rushing beneath them through the cut toward the Vinheran. Beyond even that, Diana could see a wall in the distance, just barely in her field of view.

They continued down the central platform, the sound seeming to beat away the smell now. As they walked, Diana spotted statues of monstrous creatures, beasts she didn't have a name for. Diana could make out decay on the stone faces, worn away from what wind and water had washed over them over centuries. This place was older than anything else they had passed so far, the cornerstone to the sewers, it seemed. Perhaps even older.

The thunder grew louder than Diana thought she could shout over. Water splashed the stone and she slowed down.

Getting splattered was unavoidable, but it seemed that the water was just the slightest bit cleaner here. It made little difference about the spray, but the smell of sewage was milder.

The wall stood ahead of them. They were at the base of the waterfall, two waterfalls, one to each side of the path they had been following. Why an architect would put a waterfall in a sewer was beyond her. Perhaps it was to help break down the waste that came through? At the base of the wall was an alcove that Diana guessed hid a set of stairs leading up to the top of the wall. As she peered into the alcove, she happened to find her thought correct.

Leading Kan'sa up the stairs in the dark was slow going. Diana could only take a few steps at a time, while Kan'sa insisted on long strides despite her relative blindness. It was a wonder that they only tripped up the stairs and not backward in the dim lighting. The thought became more terrifying as they approached the top of the climb.

"We should probably light that again," Diana shouted, gesturing to the torch. She then realized the movement was pointless and tapped the torch a couple times.

"With as many stairs as we went up, that would be wise." Kan'sa extended the branch out to Diana.

Diana took the torch and struck it against the ground. A few sparks bounced over the stones and the blaze pierced the darkness. They shielded their eyes, slowly readjusting to the new flame. Now that the waterfalls were cast in light, Diana could see a platform leaning out over the falls behind them. Diana turned to Kan'sa as the Hantheer's eyes finally focused. "I wonder what the builders were looking at from here."

They kept walking into the darkness. Even with the light, they couldn't find an end to the chamber. The water rushed on, the sound overpowering. Diana looked around for a side room where it might be quieter. She noticed a bridge across the channel and tugged Kan'sa along toward it. On the far side, there was a stone archway filled by a stone slab, almost invisible until the light fell on it. Dwarves often had doors like that. Kan'sa barely noticed it as they came closer, even as Diana pointed it out.

Diana pushed the door open. Its

weight meant it must be opened slowly. Kan'sa stepped into the room and lit the torches beside the entrance. Shadows were cast over the room, making the jagged objects in front of them more wicked looking.

An armory.

"Well, I guess we found the army," Diana muttered.

"We found the weapons, not the warriors," Kan'sa returned. "The halls could clearly hold many soldiers, but where did they go?"

"I haven't really seen any evidence of mana in the area either," Diana added. "I don't think there would have been an increase in magic from just lighting the place with torches. Something else had to be going on here."

Kan'sa took a few more steps into the room. "They kept this room well stocked; perhaps there was a magic forge here."

"They must have had a good quartermaster," Diana commented, looking at all the weapons. Some of them were ancient, but Diana could tell most were still sharp. Rust didn't degrade any of the blades; a sinister gleam illuminated each one.

"Perhaps he had a log," Kan'sa suggested. "About who he was arming, and why."

"A civil war is a good why."

"This seems like overkill for a civil war. A good place to hide an army, yes, but we're deep under the city. Besides," Kan'sa paused to lift one of the blades, "these are old swords. Older than eighty years."

"These don't look like any smithing style I've ever seen," Diana said.

Kan'sa pursed her lips, thinking over something for a good while, longer than Diana would have hoped. "Nor I." There was something in the statement that suggested she had a good guess though.

Diana walked around the room, searching for a desk. A banner hung on the back wall. It had faded, but the silver lily was still plain, even if the green it sat on had long faded. "I'm gonna guess this is the Lilithin's crest."

The light came closer as Kan'sa approached to look. "Lily. Lilithin. That would make sense. Aged, but not fraying. It has been here a long while, but I would not say as long as this castle has stood."

"Like less than a century?"

"I would say about twenty years less."

Diana looked up and down the wall. Surely there were some kind of records for the armory. A log of some kind. Anything that would tell them what had happened here. Diana pushed aside a pile of leather armor, hoping there might be something underneath.

They started moving away armor and shifting weapons. Looking for anything that might prove useful. The room was left overturned, but no records. Kan'sa lifted her torch up. "We should keep searching these halls. There must be other rooms like this deeper in these sewers, where soldiers would have stayed, or orders were given."

"Yeah," Diana mumbled. Something

didn't sit right. If there was nothing here, why would there be documentation anywhere else? The army had vanished, and this room was central to that army. Perhaps they wanted to hide as much evidence of their presence as they could?

The banner had been left here though. Evidence of someone connected to the Lilithin family and King Arvon harboring an army of some size remained in this room or at least knowing this room existed. Why would they want to be caught? Had they simply forgotten?

Diana walked over to the banner. She climbed onto the table and pulled the banner up. The wall was smooth, almost perfectly so. But Diana was familiar with a perfectly smooth wall. This wasn't. Not quite smooth, not to someone who knew the difference. Manually changed, not cut with precision for a smooth touch.

"This wall is altered," Diana stated, pushing lightly around the smoothed tile on the wall, trying to find a difference in texture.

"Altered?"

"It was smoothed, separate to the other walls."

"All the walls look smooth to me," Kan'sa replied, reaching forward to touch the surface Diana was prodding.

"There's looking smooth and being smooth," Diana answered. "Dwarves cut stone straight and it's like touching glass. The walls here are cut, but their tools were obviously less proficient. There are tears, little grooves, and bumps—signs of stonecutters cutting the stone after and sanding it down. It's like someone wanted to hide the blemishes of a bad cut of stone. Or a new cut."

"Smooth is smooth to me, but you seem convinced."

Diana's hands searched over it for any cut concealed by the extra attention given to the stone face. She traced it over and over, until an even square was obvious to her fingertips.

"Here, there's something here," Diana insisted. She reached into her bag. "Someone cut something in this wall."

As Diana pulled out her pen, Kan'sa asked, "What are you going to do with that?"

Diana traced a basic rune. Every schooled dwarf knew it. It was a spare key when you lost yours, or a failsafe to any lockbox. A simple command in the rune language: Unlock. The sign was simple. A horizontal line beneath an upward facing K. Diana tapped a manastone to the rune and leaned back, hoping there weren't any counter-enchantments in place.

There were none.

Diana watched the plate fall before turning to the hole in the wall. She eased her hand in. The hole wasn't deep. All it had was a stack of papers, but she had a flash of trepidation as she reached down to pull them out.

Kan'sa held the torch far enough away that it wouldn't be a risk to the parchment, but close enough that Diana still had light to read.

"7 Highsun, 689, Spoken Age," Diana read aloud, the words echoing in the halls.

"Eighty years ago, summer. About the time Lord Arvon came to the castle," Kan'sa answered, in awe. Diana was amazed as well. The chances of a dwarf coming into these halls, to find this, were slim.

Diana continued reading.

"Lord Arvon made a pact with a demon. I don't fully understand why. He mentioned an affair, but his eyes went very dark when he was asked. It is not my business though. If Lord Arvon chooses to align with demons, then I will catalog his guilt for the High Seat and submit this evidence when we return to Kalvari.

"There's not much I can do at present. The lord has assigned me to oversee the arms for this army of his, and I suppose it is an honor to be given the position if I didn't know the truth of the

matter, like the rest of the simpletons he has working down here. Perhaps it won't be as dangerous as I suspect. The lord is not so foolish as to make a pact with a truly dangerous demon.

"13 Highsun, 689, the demons have brought their own weapons. I am little more than a clerk to Lord Arvon, keeping a tally of their arms. I can't say I'm disappointed though. At least I do not have to participate in their war. I don't understand what all these soldiers are for. They're terrifying. Men and elves, but their skin is like night. Not dark like the men from Orimbela, but true blackness, like a void. Their mouths are sealed as if their bodies are hollow, yet they make noises. Terrible, horrible noises. White brands break their skin. Some have more than *others. I fear what those marks mean."*

"That's what happened to Lorraine," Diana murmured, turning to Kan'sa. The Hantheer's face was dark, like she knew something. Diana ran her tongue over her lips before pressing on.

"21 Highsun, 689, they have left. Vanished. I pray they don't return. Speaker, the things I have seen. I fear the things that marched down here, what I have been forced to do by them, will prevent me from meeting the Speaker. I fear the fiends will drag me into their legions.

"3 Sunend, 689, I cannot imagine the truth in my words. Fiends. Led by a mage demon. Why, Lord Arvon, would you make a deal with an Oediohs? I suppose it's King Arvon now though. His demons have

returned. *Blood stains their hands. Blood of the Daendran people. I have heard the lords have been wiped out, but all the other mortals here have vanished now, so I will hear no more news. I have no love for this country, but what victory is worth the savage crimes my lord would commit against his people?*

"*5 Sunend, 689, King Arvon has told me to stop writing journals on the proceedings of the army. They will be leaving soon, back to their hell, and he wants no evidence of their presence here. Part of their pact, he said. Either my journal entries end, or I will join them. Damn him.*

"*6 Sunend, 689, the king never cared about his daughter, for the court affairs she was holding here in Vinhir. He used her as an excuse to come, as an excuse to give his demon power. I heard it before I fled here. I barred the entrance. Sealed it with holy words. I will die here.*

"7 Sunend, 689, I do not fear their threats. If this ever reaches another soul, then I will have saved someone. Done the Speaker's Will. I will be leashed to their army, but perhaps another will be able to stop it because of my sacrifice."

There were two more entries when Kan'sa finally cut in. "What here interested an Oediohs though?"

"I don't think this man knew," Diana answered. "He seems like a servant to Arvon. Probably not very important if the king was fine just sending him away to deal with his army, but important enough to be trusted. Arvon wanted someone no one would miss, who would disappear with this army." She flipped through the pages again, at the choice this man had made for others over a lord. "A ghost."

"An Oediohs though," Kan'sa said with a heavy sigh.

"What do you know about demons?"

"The soldiers these entries describe, what was happening to Lorraine, we call them Meurch. Foot soldiers. Men roped into service by demons for their sins in life, or petty deals made. Our elders say that each scar on their chest marks how many centuries they will spend in service."

"*Centuries*?"

"Demons are not well-known for their kindness," Kan'sa replied, leaving a sour taste in Diana's mouth. No, they certainly weren't. "This man is admirable though. Leaving these notes even though he knew it would cost him his life. A shame we will never know his name."

"There is probably a record of the staff kept somewhere," Diana commented.

"If King Arvon went as far as forming a demon pact to wipe out the Daendran lords and to mask everything they have hidden already, I doubt destroying this man's records would have been difficult. Like you said, they would have wanted someone easily forgotten so no one would question altered records."

The thought was hollow but right. There wasn't anything they could do for the man. They could only use this information to stop an army. A demon army.

"What is an Oediohs though?"

Kan'sa swallowed and paced away.

"Oediohses are the most powerful mages of demons. There are few demons more powerful. We know they are limited in number, but not how many. They are beasts of raw magic, trapped in human skins twisted to cover broken forms. What the limit to their power is though, we do not know. Beyond cult worship of their kind, only the Blesseds have viewed these particular monsters and lived."

"And Arvon made a pact with one?"

"Coerced seems more like it. We have history of his family's deeds. His father was a kind mortal, and championed peace between Kalmaran and its neighbors. To turn on such a legacy so suddenly sounds like possession to me."

"Can Oediohses do that?" Diana felt a chill run through her body.

"We do not know what limitations they might have with their magic," Kan'sa answered grimly. "Possession would not be their most terrifying ability. It would have been done slowly, so no one would have noticed until the deed was done."

Diana gripped the paper and found herself shaking. She tried to steady her hand, but with little success. Kan'sa stepped forward and held Diana's wrist. "It will be all right, friend. You do not have to keep reading."

"No, we've gotten this far, and it looks like there are only two more entries," Diana answered. She didn't shirk Kan'sa's comfort though.

Kan'sa nodded. "All right, if you are sure."

Clearing her throat, Diana read on.

STOLEN SECRET

"*8 Sunend, 689, I hung a banner when this all began, a bit of color I said, for the underground. The beasts did not demand its removal and so I kept it. I have carved a vault behind it though. I modeled it after the dwarven chests I have seen during my travels. Master crafts, and I am grateful I had the privilege to see the dwarven handiwork. Mine is small, but I pray it will go unnoticed. They may not know it, but those craftsmen will now save my account of the horrors I have seen.*

"*They will break down the door. I can hear them, but I know the Speaker will give me until then. To clear away the sanded stone and the debris so that I may preserve the Will from my hidden chamber. I pray the Speaker can hear me here.*

"*To whomever finds this,*

understand this: An Oediohs has made a pact with King Arvon to give Daendra to the Lilithin family for one hundred years in exchange for the Astorian ruins this army gathered in. If anyone contests the king's reign, the demon army will rise again to quell it. In exchange, King Arvon will give the demon Vinhir in a hundred years' time. I will never know if he succeeds, but I do not believe that the king will die until he has. The Mage has an unholy nature in that way.

"I cannot imagine what an Oediohs would do to our reality, but I pray you will not find out. I do not understand the ruins here. Perhaps answers lie in Astior, in their oldest histories. Speaker help you find the truth that I couldn't. Warn any rebels against attacking the city. The demons

appeared only briefly to kill the lords. If they took the city, the war between Daendra and Hanmark would destroy half the nation. Even I could not wish that on them.

"I pray Vinhir lives though."

Diana paused, taking a deep breath. She was trembling. Kan'sa started to comment, but Diana shook her head. "There is one more. I don't think it's even dated."

Kan'sa gripped Diana a little tighter. Diana didn't watch as Kan'sa turned to face the door. She held the page close enough to read as the torch was blown out. *"I will not last. The demons have stopped. They have gone. The Mage itself attacks the door. It has not gone."*

CHAPTER 8
THE DEMON MAGE

Diana's hand shook. "Kan'sa, we need to go."

Kan'sa was stiff. Diana swallowed, turning to face the entrance as well. She wished she could close her eyes, but it wouldn't have done any good.

A voice crawled through the room, finding all the light and snuffing out. In its wake was a different kind of light. It was more like the sense of light, like the world had become silhouetted by the force of the creature. "He was pathetic when he went. Thank you though. I can finally wipe this from history."

"Speaker," Diana swore. Or prayed. She wasn't sure. It wasn't mortal, but it was pretending to be. Flesh was stretched over a humanoid shape, but there were seams where something dark slipped through. Its face was hardly that, three cuts in its skin where that blackness emitted as if those holes were orifices. She could feel the magic coming from its body. That magic slowly collected, leaving mana to condense into manastones. The clear crystals clinked off on the floor, a dozen little chimes in the darkness.

But nothing compared to the

massive portals it had torn open to bring forth an army beyond the chamber. It felt like the world had been ripped apart, even from here, like its skin had been yanked away, leaving only dark red wounds where it should have been.

"I'm afraid they can't hear you here either," the demon said. Its voice was like salt and ice on an open wound. It burned beneath Diana's skin. "Shame, they'll miss their lovely World Walker. Perhaps the runt as well."

Diana grimaced, but her fear would do nothing. Kan'sa described this monster as death incarnate. It would take a miracle for them to escape. "Is Lorraine one of your lackeys then?"

"Hm, that fool made a deal too long ago, idle worship. I have no interest in the adoration of mortals. But she appears to have had her uses." The Oediohs chuckled. "Maybe I'll send her to haunt you when her soul crawls back to my reaches. But I need not send for someone to lure you here or scare you from this city. You were set on finding this place from the moment you left Dane, and no intervention would have stayed you."

"Who does this prick think he is?" Diana growled, terrified by her bravery.

"You'll find out soon," the demon purred. "But for now, you have brought a rebellion to the gates of Vinhir. I have pacts to fulfill."

The creature slinked out, slow and confident, as if it had graced them with some cruel mercy by leaving them alive. Diana shuddered at the sight.

Kan'sa pressed the torch into Diana's hand. "I will cover your escape."

"What? Kan'sa, you can't!" Diana called, her voice cutting out as her eyes fell on the Demon Mage, but the Hantheer was already headed for the door.

"This is my duty, Diana. Do not let our sacrifices be wasted."

Diana gripped the pages in her hand. It couldn't take Kan'sa. It wouldn't take Kan'sa. Diana watched Kan'sa rush the door, drawing her bow and nocking an arrow. "Fiend, I am this time's World Walker. I come on behalf of the Speaker. Your presence is not permitted."

The Mage didn't even turn its head to show it was listening. It merely walked up to the platform above the stairs, stepping up before its portal. Light started to appear in the halls, unnatural and green.

Kan'sa let an arrow fly, aimed with the same accuracy that had brought home a creature every evening while Diana tried to get into the mages' guild. It embedded itself into the Mage's shoulder, but it did not wince. Slowly, it turned toward its attacker and smiled.

"You think yourself brave, Hantheer?" the Mage asked, making no effort to raise its voice, yet Diana heard it clearly. "Do you think your actions will matter? You act on your god's whim, for what? Peace? Did you ever believe you would achieve that? You are a fool, dreaming about a fool's hope."

"And you are a sin upon this earth, and you will not remain," Kan'sa returned, raising her voice over the waterfalls, drawing another arrow. "My faith guides me."

"Your faith will kill you."

Diana shuddered to watch as she leaned on the armory's doorway, but she couldn't tear herself from where she stood. Kan'sa loosed arrow after arrow, each finding their mark but none seeming to affect the beast that stood before them. The Oediohs grinned as Kan'sa notched her last shot. "What will you do, deer child?"

"Hold you from your pact," Kan'sa answered. "If you cannot fulfill your pact with the king, then your purchase into this land will be broken. You will not lay a hand on Daendran blood so long as I still stand."

"Admirable, but do you even know how long you must face me? I can hear the lords convening now. There will be bloodshed for Lord Frederick Hawkfel's treason. Arvon will not cross me. And you cannot prevent it here in the sewers of the city. You will stop nothing."

"You mean to frighten me?"

"Indeed, foolish child, you stand bef—"

Kan'sa's arrow embedded itself between the Oediohs's eye slits. That staggered it. Kan'sa drew her hunting dagger, holding it at the ready but not attacking yet. Stalling, for Diana. The Hantheer's retort cut as sharp as the knife would have, "It is a meager *attempt*."

Diana felt pride swell in her chest. Kan'sa, you crazy deer woman, she thought, you might have a chance at this. This insane, religious, fearsome woman was someone Diana had the privilege to call her friend. And in the face of a demon, an enemy almost none had faced, that woman had taunted it.

"Leave, Diana," Kan'sa ordered. "It is stunned, but for how long, I cannot say."

"You have to get out of here too," Diana replied. "Without you, how will—"

"You have the journal. That is more than enough. Now leave!"

Kan'sa met Diana's eyes, their fear meeting for a moment. Kan'sa smiled. "Speaker guide you, Diana Silverwell. I am not afraid, and you should not be either. We walk the Speaker's path. Perhaps you will change the world."

"That's supposed to be your job, savior," Diana returned, swallowing the lump in her throat.

Kan'sa closed her eyes and turned to

face the Oediohs. It was starting to tremble, returning from its daze. One by one, the arrows fell from its skin, leaving trails of ivory blood and black miasmas in its wake.

Diana didn't wait to be ordered again. She couldn't fight. What was she going to do against a demon? Leaving Kan'sa tore her heart in two, but someone had to survive this mess. She prayed to the Speaker that Kil'thian had sensed the disturbance, that he would find them in the sewers. Even the hart had to swallow his pride for this threat. He wouldn't leave Kan'sa to die.

As Diana sped down the stairs in the green light, she heard the last arrow fall with a clatter to the stone floor. The demon laughed. It laughed a horrible, wretched sound, like the voice of plague with the cut of a rusted scythe. Diana felt like she was going to vomit. She gripped the wall to steady herself. Images of the guardsman from the highway flashed in her mind. Her brain was seared with the image of his death, with the way his body had shook from Diana's spell. Lorraine's corpse, the blood on Kil'thian's antlers. Her eyes flashed red. And the demon kept laughing.

"You dare challenge me! You are a fool! A speck, a rodent, and soon you will be ash," the Mage bellowed. Its voice commanded the space. How did no one else hear it? Was anyone coming?

Diana forced herself down the stairs. She forced herself to remember everything Kan'sa had told her about being worthy of living. She forced herself to keep going, even as she heard Kan'sa behind her, just barely over the waterfalls crashing around her.

"You will not proceed. This realm is under the guidance of the Speaker, and we are its shepherds." Diana heard metal clashing against metal. The real fight had begun. Each strike reverberated through the halls. The blades locked and ground against each other. "Your violation of this world will not continue."

"And where is your Speaker now?"

Diana heard the roar as she raced down the steps. The end of the stairwell was in sight. All that remained was the flight across the long hall to the narrow passage they'd come through, and back out to the sun. It sounded so much easier in her head. She almost laughed at the idea.

Leaping from the stairs, Diana ran as fast as her legs could carry her. Why did the hall have to be so goddamn long? Something clattered in front of her, the sound absorbed by the waterfalls. Diana saw the glint of something on the floor, but she realized too late what it was. Kan'sa's hunting knife.

Time stopped at that moment. Diana's body was frozen as she stared at the sight. She turned to see the Oediohs knock Kan'sa's bleeding body over the edge of the extended platform. The long, slender body fell, but Kan'sa didn't flail. She was thrown toward Diana, toward the stone floor and not the water, turned only by gravity in her plummet to a certain death.

The words that left Diana's mouth were inaudible as a bugle sounded from behind her, crying out as clearly as the Oediohs had spoken. Hooves thudded by before the dwarf knew what was happening. Diana blinked and suddenly Kil'thian was there, buckling under the weight of the falling Hantheer. The hart slid back several feet, Kan'sa thrown over his side. Her right arm was bent at a horrible angle.

Diana rushed to her friend. Kil'thian slowly stood up, sore but not wounded. He snorted at Diana's approach. "Is she alive?"

Kil'thian nudged Kan'sa's body with his nose. She released a breath, weak and raspy. She was alive, but barely. Diana looked into Kil'thian's amber eyes. "Do I even need to tell you to get her out of here?"

The hart started to stand, but stopped, pointing out across the hall. Diana turned and saw a shadow taking shape twenty feet away from her. She didn't need anyone to tell her what it was going to be in a few moments.

"Di-an-a," Kan'sa coughed. Her eyes were bleary, blood running from her nose and three long, crooked cuts on her chest, right forearm, and right thigh. Diana turned to her friend and shook her head. Kan'sa coughed again, blood on her lips. "It-it must...fulfill—" She gasped in pain, "its pact...or it'll..."

Kan'sa lost consciousness. Diana turned around to face the shadow. The demon's pact with the king. A pact to raise an army to prevent the Lilithin family from losing the throne if Vinhir was attacked. A pact that would be broken if Arvon stepped down and no army appeared to save him. No one of Daendran blood could die, that's what Kan'sa had said.

"Do not trifle with things you don't

understand, dwarf." The shadow had finished materializing. Diana had to act now, or they would never have a chance.

"Killy, whenever you can, you get her to the throne room," Diana ordered in a low voice. The Oediohs could hear her regardless and grinned as Diana continued to explain, "She is Lord Hawkfel's sign, which means the Speaker supports him. Just get her there. If anyone tries to argue with her—" Diana's fists clenched as she met Kil'thian's eyes. "You show those fuckers why you're the damned sign of the Speaker."

Kil'thian snorted. He understood the necessity of getting Kan'sa out alive, of getting support to Lord Hawkfel before hell broke loose in the Council. The hart would fly faster than Diana ever could with the notes. But as the hart stood to run, a fireball landed inches before them, searing the stone. The Oediohs loomed closer, another ball of dark magic swelling in its palm. Kil'thian stood ready, waiting for the moment to start his flight when the Mage would not strike him down. And even if the notes burned with Diana here, Kan'sa would know the truth. She would be able to find out more. This was her quest, her duty, and Diana was going to make sure her friend saw it to the end.

"What will you do, stoneheart?" the demon asked, prying the slur from Diana's mind. Diana felt its claws sinking into her, searching for secrets to bend against her. It found only the slur before her race's magical immunities pushed it out. "You trifle with the very balance of magic, proclaiming yourself a mage when your kind cannot feel the surge of mana in the world." It grinned, its fangs like daggers in its mouth, ugly and pointed. "Perhaps I will drag you into my legion when you die, prying at magic you have no right to wield. Perhaps we will be allies in another life."

Diana curled her lip. "Go to hell."

"Why are you even here, dwarf? You left your life in Dane for what? A quest for a god you barely believe in. Now your god betrays you, and your friend. Your romanticism and wanderlust, your pathetic sense of adventure has brought you to your tomb." The Mage stalked toward her. "It seems foolish to offer you a deal. You would throw it away in the name of righteousness. I see why you followed her so blindly to your death."

The Oediohs stopped and paced. It

even dared to turn away from Diana. Diana knew it was because the demon didn't need to see her to kill her, and it was goading her with it. Diana shoved the pages into her sack and fished her hand around, searching for the right scroll. The demon continued, "You are nothing, dwarf. Dust and ash and nothing. I will step over you and into this world after my years of waiting, and there isn't a thing you can do to stop me."

This one. Diana gripped the parchment. "You sure like to monologue." Kan'sa give her courage, she was about to do something incredibly stupid.

It snickered at her. Diana's body was like jelly, but the warmth of Kil'thian behind her kept her going. "You think you stand a chance here, don't you?"

Diana snapped the wax seal, now

properly labeled. The energy surged on her palm, never passing inside, and she threw the surge toward the demon. It laughed, that horrible, awful bellow. "Not even a decent scroll, mage."

"Do you know why most dwarves don't know how to write lightning spell scrolls?" Diana asked, standing slightly. *Speaker, let this work.*

"Oh, enlighten me, dwarf."

The roof broke. The sunlight burned Diana's eyes and she had to turn away as the lightning struck the Oediohs. It writhed in the light and shuddered from the electrocution. Kil'thian took the chance. In a heartbeat, he was gone from the hall, Kan'sa on his back.

Diana coughed as the dust settled. "Because the spearhead has to come from somewhere. Not great for roofs."

The echo of Kil'thian's hooves diminished, fleeing the moment the Oediohs became stunned. The demon, half frozen, turned its eyes toward the tunnel, roaring but unable to move. Its eyes fell on Diana, who had made no move to flee. As those eyes, filled with ire and rage, fell on her, it finally dawned on her that she probably should. Beyond royally pissing off a demon, she had just punched a hole in the ceiling, and the falling rocks were about to compound.

She wished her legs were longer. Diana ran forward. She bent and grabbed Kan'sa's hunting knife, only inches from where the Oediohs was standing. One hand on the knife, while the other searched her bag for another scroll, Diana ran as fast as her body could carry her out of the tunnel.

The green light faded, and Diana was thrown into darkness. Her eyes struggled to adjust, but something blotted out the small glimpses she got. She didn't slow down to let them adjust. She just kept running.

Stones toppled behind her as she rushed the bridge at the far end of the hall. She was in the tunnel once more. The darkness that leaked from the Oediohs still chased her, but it slowed, slipping through the rumble now blocking her path back. Behind her, she heard the world rip open, like stone and fabric yanked apart. Something roared in that beyond, something Diana realized was a trumpet. She could hear the steady beats of a marching force, but she didn't dare look back to count. All she could do was listen as the sounds of footfall multiplied fourfold every second. Demons, pouring out to assault Vinhir.

Diana passed through a gate. She grabbed the door as she went, throwing it closed behind her. Her hand found a fire scroll, and she threw it at the metal gate without aiming. She could hear steam hissing as she ran.

Her chest was tight and her breathing short. Her legs wanted to give, but she refused to slow down. Stopping now meant she was going to die. She didn't think about how likely it was that she would survive.

Another gate. Diana threw an ice spell at it as she passed, the gate hardening under the cold and then the spears of icicles spread out. At least a few monsters would be caught on that.

So her flight went. Another gate, another scroll. Some were left in flames, others coated in ice, others crackling with electricity. Eventually though, Diana ran out of scrolls to use. She kept throwing the gates back as she ran, and she kept running. It was getting harder and harder to block out the sound of whatever was pursuing her in the darkness. And the more she ran, the louder the sound got. The army was growing, and she didn't want to see what marched out.

Daylight was ahead. Diana summoned all her strength to make the last stretch. She didn't know why she felt like the sun would save her, it just seemed like the sort of thing that saved people in that moment.

She closed her eyes and left the tunnel behind. The sunlight pierced her eyelids, but it was better than being blind for several minutes. Diana collided with something.

"Didn't know there was a dwarf city under Vinhir."

"You idiot, that's the sewers."

"Dwarves live in the sewers?"

Diana opened her eyes. Two soldiers with Hawkfel's crest stood in front of her. She let out a deep breath and fell to her knees. "Thank the Speaker."

"What are you all out of breath about?"

A roar erupted from the tunnel. All eyes fell on the entrance, which seemed to expand as they stood there, listening to the pounding of footsteps.

"What is that?"

"Demons," Diana managed, her chest struggling to fill itself.

"Demons! What were you doing in the sewers?"

"If you think I brought them, you're pretty slow," Diana grumbled, rolling to her feet.

The footsteps thundered closer. The guards turned to each other. "What do we do?"

"We fight them."

The thought struck her. Diana leaped up. "No, don't! Get out of here! Now!"

"Want to take on the legion on your own, huh?"

Diana was baffled. She almost commented on his idiocy but elected against it. "King Arvon, he made a pact with a demon to keep any rebellions in check. If they kill you, if they kill anyone of Daendran blood, then that army keeps coming."

"What are you talking about? The king making a pact with a demon?"

She had to get them out of here. Diana roared, "Lord Frederick is in danger. It's an attack on him. Someone has to warn him."

"You go, we'll fight these monsters."

Diana felt like her head was going to explode. "I just ran out of a demon infested-sewer and now you want me to run all the way—"

The footsteps were getting louder. They were joined by the steady, slow stomps of something much, much larger. Diana turned toward the tunnel again. How was she going to get these morons to leave?

"That sounds like an-an awful big demon."

"We're Lord Hawkfel's men. We don't run from demons. We have the Speaker on our side."

Diana pressed her lips together. They weren't going to budge. Maybe she could talk their way out of this. The Oediohs had loved running its mouth. Perhaps these would be the same way.

Out of the tunnel emerged two ebony skinned soldiers. They were just as the notes had described, fully charred versions of Lorraine. Ebony in skin with white scars running down their bodies. They carried swords like the blades in the armory, honed to a lethal point.

Clutching Kan'sa's dagger in her

hand, Diana let the sides of the hilt burn against her palm. She felt weak and close to fainting, but she wasn't going to get this far and die now. She suddenly felt resolve pooling inside her. Diana prayed it would last long enough for her to see tomorrow.

A leg came through the shadow of the tunnel. A huge, plated leg that was the size of a tree trunk. It had a wicked gleam to it. To Diana, it looked like countless iron shields gorged into some huge beast's body, over and over again until all the flesh was covered by the massive sheets of metal.

The next leg came out of the darkness, and then the torso, then the arms, and finally, the huge helmeted head. The beast had to stoop to leave the eight-foot-high tunnel. Now it stood at its full height and bellowed.

Diana and the guards covered their ears at the roar. The guards trembled. Diana was beyond trembling. She was so tired of all this demon shit that she stopped caring, and she was keeping that attitude until she slept or died. She preferred the former.

"What was that you said about not getting killed?"

"That would be ideal over the us dying option," Diana shouted back.

It was three on three. Well, two and a half. Or maybe four to— Diana pushed aside the odds. She had no idea how to fight that behemoth at the entrance of the tunnel.

The two smaller demons charged first, their swords raised, and shouting somehow despite their lack of mouths. It was just another layer of muscle in place of a tongue or teeth.

STOLEN SECRET

Diana heard the guards back away from the fight a step, but when Diana didn't move, they reluctantly stood their ground. They shifted awkwardly behind her. This was going to end poorly. The guards' blades met the demons' weapons. Diana threw Kan'sa's dagger at one of the demon's heads. It grazed the monster, but that gave the guard enough time to swing high and sever the beast's head. He turned to join his companion's fight.

With the two focused, Diana turned toward the huge lumbering demon as it finally began moving from the tunnel's entrance. Without any weapons and no scrolls left to use—not to mention she was about to pass out from exhaustion—it was a miracle she was still standing. After the lightning spearhead scroll, it was a wonder

Diana had any more miracles left.

A bell sounded in Vinhir. It cut through even the massive demon's roar. As the beast they fought fell, the two guards turned toward the sound. Diana watched the massive demon in front of her, waiting for it to turn its attention to the more present issue. But the demon didn't move. It stood there, frozen.

And suddenly, it was gone.

Just vanished entirely. Diana turned to the guards behind her.

"Then he did it. He said the bell would ring," one spoke. "One if Arvon stepped down."

Diana let out a sigh of relief. The rebellion was over. Kan'sa had gotten to the throne room, had stopped King Arvon. "She did it.”

     And then she was surrounded by darkness.

CHAPTER 9
TO THE VICTOR

Sunlight. Soft morning sunlight trickled in through the windows. Diana blinked awake, moaned and rolled over. It wasn't sunny in Dane.

Then it all came back to her.

She sat up and looked around the room. It was big, painted in pastels and golds—fancy and wealthy. But she was alive. Also, the bed was the softest mattress she had ever slept on. She pressed herself into it another inch as memories flooded her mind of the past three months.

The room was too big for Diana. It was nice to have space, but there was just so much. She felt like she was back in the hall in the sewers. Too much space and nothing to fill it. Perhaps it would have been better with taller people, but then it would have been less of a bedroom.

Pulling herself out of bed, Diana walked to one of the tall windows. She gasped as she looked out across the cityscape of Vinhir, glistening in the morning light.

"Am I in the castle?" Diana asked, looking around on the horizon for taller structures. There were none. Diana leaned back from the window and scanned the room. She found her bag, half-empty without her scrolls. The journal from the vaults was gone. A pit formed in Diana's stomach as worry filled her thoughts that, after all this, the entries had been lost. Then she shook her head and let the thought go. Even if they had, four people had seen the demons. Two of them were soldiers for a notable lord, who must still have some part of his title since she was here and not in a jail cell. It was more likely that the journal had been taken for evidence against King Arvon.

Diana found her clothes washed and dried in a dresser. She pulled out a long tunic and some of her looser pants. She wasn't interested in dressing up after what had happened in the sewer. Right now, she just wanted to rest and breathe easy.

Dressed, Diana opened the door to her room. Outside was a guard. He jumped up and saluted. "Lady Silverwell, you're awake!"

"Yeah, hello," Diana answered, closing the bedroom door behind her. "You don't have to worry about all that lady business. It's just Diana."

"Yes, ma'am."

Completely missed the point, Diana thought, but she simply smiled. "How long was I asleep?"

"Two days, ma'am, but you're fine otherwise," the guard answered. "The court's doctor personally oversaw your health, since our healer was occupied with the World Walker's."

"Kan'sa!" Diana exclaimed, ignoring that a healer wouldn't have been any good for her anyway. "Is she all right?"

"Ma'am..."

"Can I see her at least?" Don't die on me, Kan'sa, not after all this.

"I would ask Ms. Eveningstorm. She is most likely in the throne room, assisting King Frederick with the transition."

"King Frederick?" Diana asked, scowling. What happened to not vying for power?

"I think Ms. Eveningstorm can answer your questions better. She will be in the main hall." He pointed down the hall, and gestured to the left, not that it did any good this far away from the door that he meant. Diana thanked him and started walking.

The halls were just as ornate as the bedroom Diana had been given. There were still logs and cobbled stone bricks. Diana didn't think a building could be Daendran without the two. They liked the hunting lodge feel, even in their grander buildings. Still, this wing of the castle seemed to favor light wood over the dark wood, giving it a regal appearance without losing the favored design of the country. Paintings hung on the walls, highlighting artists from across the continent. Diana guessed the paintings had been brought in by the previous rulers.

It was obvious which doors the guard had meant. They had a huge golden frame, far more extravagant than the other portals. Diana pushed them open, wishing more people would consider the weight of doors for shorter guests. Then again, she figured dwarves hadn't frequently been welcomed to banquets in Vinhir.

Beyond was a great hall. Diana entered on a narrow floor snaking above the main chamber, giving her a grand view of the room as she made her way toward the stairs behind the throne. It was much like the great hall in Hawkfel in that it seemed to serve as both a throne room and a banquet space. Diana could see the even larger doors to the entrance of the castle at the far end, with only a single archway separating the hall from a small anteroom. At least, it was small compared to the grand hall. It was about the size of Diana's bedroom.

"Ah, our heroic dwarf is awake!"

That accent was familiar. Daendran with a hint of Kalmaranian. Diana took a few steps down the staircase. Claire and Emilie Eveningstorm were waiting at the base of the stairs, smiling at Diana's approach. Emilie had her arms folded across her chest, smiling brightly. Claire peered up over her clipboard, a small but happy smile on her face.

"You and Kan'sa have been busy. I got a very interesting message from a young man from the merchants' guild," Claire commented, looking down at her clipboard. "Rumor has it a hart broke into the mage's guild three days ago."

"But of course, the only hart in Vinhir has been resting in the Royal Stables for days," Emilie added with a grin and a conspirator's wink. "He couldn't have."

"It's good to see you again," Diana said. And it was true. Even if it wasn't Kan'sa, seeing someone she knew instead of smiling servants and guards made this morning less confusing.

Emilie nudged her twin with her shoulder. "See, I told you she liked us." Claire pressed her lips together in a thin line. Emilie laughed. "Oh, don't mind her, she's still embarrassed about asking for a job."

"Emilie!"

Diana laughed, which led Emilie to laugh as well and Claire to blush profusely. Diana shook her head. "It's fine. We were all a little drunk, and Kan'sa was struggling with a lot of questions. But I think she might reconsider now." Claire let out a breath of relief and nodded. Diana put her hands up. "I'm not promising you a job. We may not be in Daendra for much longer. I know Kan'sa wanted to see Hanmark, if she's still..." She lost her voice.

Emilie and Claire exchanged a look.

Claire started, "The speaker of Speaker is fine, my friend. At least, she is alive."

"The guard outside my door made it sound like she wasn't all right."

"Well, I wouldn't say she's all right," Emilie replied, crossing her arms. "She broke her arm, pretty serious fracture. The healer is taking it slowly to make sure the bone heals correctly. Last thing we'd want is a World Walker with a useless arm."

Diana felt her whole body relax. "Then she's safe."

"Stable and resting, yes. How long the recovery will take, we can ask the healer when he is free," Claire explained. "In the meantime, I must ask how you are feeling. The king has several questions for you considering what you saw in the sewers. Chiefly, he is concerned about a demon army appearing in his city."

"If both of those soldiers with me were fine, then the Oediohs broke its pact with King Arvon. If no one died during the Council, then they didn't step in like the pact would have required them to, breaking it," Diana replied. "So, it should be gone now?"

"That's the theory, but this is an Oediohs," Emilie answered. "You don't have to be one of those demon specialists to know we know next to nothin' about them."

"A demonologist," Claire suggested for her sibling.

"Yeah, that."

Claire sighed. "I hope you don't mind that we recovered the journal entries from your pack. It helped us affirm without any doubt that Arvon should step down and give the crown to King Hawkfel."

"About that. Can someone explain how that happened?" Diana asked, though it seemed more like a statement. "He told Kan'sa he wouldn't take the crown."

"You should have seen it!" Emilie shouted, already laughing. "That big, ol' hart came plowing in here like he was on fire. Kan'sa barely got out 'Pact with a demon!' before she passed out again. Then the whole court was yelling at each other about who was really a devout Listener, and whether or not that was a real Hantheer and what was a big elk like that doing in the court. Your hart just about skewered the lord of Westcreek."

"It was Gosmire, but yes, there was quite a scene."

Even in a state of emergency, Kil'thian was still too proud to let someone call him anything less than a hart. Diana couldn't be too angry. He had outrun a demon army and, by proxy, saved her life.

"In the end, King Arvon stepped down. He died on the spot, and the court believes from guilt of the accusations. Between the journal entries and the testimonies of the two guards with you, it was a brief matter of convincing the other lords of this. Thus came the matter of naming a new king," Claire explained. "Most of the lords named under Arvon had made plans to leave Daendra with what remains of his family, giving up their titles. In their absence, this made a vote to name King Hawkfel as such fairly simple, since those who remained already supported him."

"Peacefully," Diana answered, remembering the conversation back in

Hawkfel.

"King Hawkfel is an honorable man," Claire replied.

"Not that it was ever in doubt," Emilie added, leaning back and tightening her arms across her chest.

Diana grinned. "No, of course not."

"How do you feel though? That question seems to have been lost in our conversation," Claire inquired.

Forced to think about, Diana just shrugged. "Fine, I guess."

"Fine?" Emilie asked, chuckling a little. "You faced an Oediohs and lived and all you have to say is fine?"

"I guess? Guilty about the hole in the road I made," Diana suggested.

"That did scare a few merchants, but it is repairable," Claire stated. "Still, no one has survived an encounter with the Oediohses. The only reason we know anything about them is from the Blesseds seeing visions of their kind."

"First a mage, then surviving a lord of all evil magics." Emilie whistled. "What law of nature will you break next?"

"Give me a day and I'll tell you," Diana quipped.

"Before you run off on your next escapade, perhaps you would like to eat?" Claire said. "I'm sure the cook staff would be happy to prepare something and, by the time you finish, Kan'sa will likely be done with her treatment for the day."

The Eveningstorms led Diana into a servant's dining room just off the kitchen. Claire tried very hard to glean answers about what the Oediohs had said, while

Emilie jokingly inquired about the fight. By the end of it, the stablemaster had it sounding like Diana single-handedly defeated a whole legion of demons. Given a few years, that would probably end up being the story that was told. But a part of Diana didn't mind the idea of that.

Filled with a savory roast and more beer than Claire was happy about, the three headed for the healer's ward. Claire and Emilie introduced Diana to the royal healer, though introductions were hardly necessary. Diana was the only dwarf in the castle, and probably the last person the healer would be seeing frequently. The twins said their goodbyes and went on to their respective duties. After that, the healer briefly explained Kan'sa's condition before directing Diana to a room down the hall.

"Just a moment."

Pausing their conversation, the healer and Diana looked up. In the doorway stood Frederick. The crown on his brow was simple, a small gold circlet with an emerald set at its center. He wore no cape or other formal gowns. A man of his people still.

"If I might have a word with Ms. Silverwell before she leaves," King Hawkfel asked.

Bowing his head, the healer walked off. Diana forced herself away from the directions she had been given and walked over to the new king. "You made some big promises to still have that crown."

"A choice of my people, not mine," Frederick answered. "And I've already spoken to Kan'sa about this. She has given her blessing. I will bear both with honor."

He motioned briefly to his crown.

Folding her arms, Diana nodded. "I think you'll do fine. But can I give you a piece of advice?"

"Please do," Frederick answered, genuine interest across his face.

"Stick to one mug of the dwarven drink," Diana stated. "I'm sure you're about to be involved with all kinds of political nonsense, and as much as I would get drunk in a heartbeat there, you might want to reconsider making intoxicated decisions."

The king paused, surprised. And then his lips cracked. He laughed, a deep, hard laugh, almost making him double over. With a sigh, Frederick shook his head. "You are a marvel, Diana. Do you fear anything?"

"Taxes," Diana lied. After the past few days she had had, there was too much to list.

Again, Frederick chuckled. "I'm afraid I do need those."

With a shrug, Diana answered, "I don't have a home or business. Don't think I qualify." She smirked but curbed her wit. "What about Hawkfel? Who becomes the lord of it now?"

"I do have a family. My nephew will be stepping in."

"Right," Diana murmured, looking away. The reality of this conversation became increasingly tense as she realized she was really speaking to a king. "Well, I need to see Kan'sa."

As Diana turned away, Frederick called after her, "Diana, I will be needing new members in my court. I lack an experienced master of the arcane, and I believe you have quite a mastery of the subject matter. It would be an honor to have your council here, and to perhaps bridge the rift between your homeland and Daendra."

Stopping, Diana turned the idea over in her head. An honor and a title given genuinely. Without looking back, Diana smiled. She continued down the hall, saying back, "I need to go."

Diana opened the door to Kan'sa's room. It was smaller, but a similar style to Diana's with the addition of a balcony. The wind pooled in the door to the outside. Kan'sa was asleep in a chair, partially reclined and enjoying the early daylight. Her arm was bound by a splint. As the door closed behind Diana, Kan'sa's eyes flickered open.

"Diana!" Kan'sa started to get up,

but then winced and sat back down.

Jogging across the room, Diana greeted her friend. "I heard about your arm. Just relax."

Kan'sa nodded, leaning back in her chair. Diana took a few cautious steps out onto the balcony. She was still getting used to being on the surface and being up so high wasn't making the resurfacing any easier.

"They told me you were all right, but when I couldn't see you, part of me was still worried," Kan'sa said softly, like she was having trouble finding her voice. "It is good to see you again."

"I'm glad you're alive," Diana answered, remembering Kan'sa falling and the fear that had gripped her in that moment.

"And I you."

Diana forgot Kan'sa didn't know if Diana was going to survive either. She had been so focused on trying to save herself and praying for her friend, she hadn't had time to think about it.

"Yeah, but I got out looking prettier," Diana retorted playfully. Kan'sa laughed. Her voice was weak, but still warm, despite it all. Kan'sa was still Kan'sa.

Kan'sa frowned and set her head back. "My quest has become far more difficult. There was a demon here, an Oediohs, for eighty years, and no World Walker. Why? Why would the Speaker do nothing about such a threat? Why was it here? What answers await me, and what roads must I take to find them? I fear I will only find greater horrors in knowing that truth."

"You can say that again."

"I fear the path ahead of me will be long and dangerous," Kan'sa went on. "I cannot ask you to join me. You know what I must face, that there will be more and worse than what we faced here."

"All the more reason to come along," Diana answered. Kan'sa lifted her head and looked Diana in the eyes. "What? If we're going to be fair, my one spell stunned that guy longer than all your arrows. You need me. All that training, and I get us out of there on luck."

"Diana."

Diana shrugged. "Besides, other than all the crazy rides and court politics and demons, these have been some of the best days in my life. And if I'm gone, who is going to help you reason anyone over to your cause? You drag people into sewers and have them fight demons. You need a good spokesperson."

"I cannot think of anyone who would willingly run toward fighting demons over the favor of a king," Kan'sa replied.

"So, he mentioned that offer?" Diana inquired.

"He did," Kan'sa answered. She waited, curiosity clear on her face.

"I'm not taking it," Diana stated. "All the honor in the world wouldn't get me to stay in the middle of any court wearing suits all day. One night with you was enough." She smirked, softly. When Kan'sa chuckled, Diana guessed joking about that night was safe.

A silence settled over them. Kan'sa drifted back into her thoughts. Diana twitched her fingers, wondering what to say next.

"You're going to chase after that thing, aren't you?"

Kan'sa sighed. "There was a demon walking through this world, a powerful one at that. I have more questions now than I did when I came here. But I have two leads. Hanmark and Astior. And so much else. Where was it? What did it do while it was here? Who else was under its spell?"

"Then we find someone else to help us look. Have Claire look into it. She and Emilie could have a legion of courtiers out spreading the news of the World Walker in a matter of days, with the right funding," Diana answered. "Between them, we could get news about potential information *and* have time to be out looking for answers about what big-and-ugly was up to." Diana pointed down, despite the fact that the sewer was now void of demons. The gesture was still obvious.

Kan'sa shook her head but smiled. "I haven't the slightest idea on how to fund an operation like that."

"Between the High Seat and the mages' guild, presuming I'm still in it, we should be fine," Diana said. "You can leave the finances to me. I was practically born in the merchants' guild, after all. Gotta earn my keep somehow."

"Stunning demon lords and saving kingdoms not enough for you?"

Diana grinned. "It's just the start."

EPILOGUE

It was cool. The moon was waning. Kan'sa stepped out on the balcony, staring up at the stars. She was tired, but now it was from spending too long around diplomats instead of from the stiffness in her arm. After two weeks, the healer had decided it was fully mended. She and Diana were planning on heading to Hanmark soon, with full support from the newly coronated King Hawkfel.

Much of the past two weeks had been answering questions, followed by more feasts than was good for anyone. Diana had finally gotten drunk, properly dwarven drunk. The king had bought real dwarven beer this time, on her recommendation. By dessert, she was a belligerent mess. Neither of them were graceful drunks.

Kan'sa laughed, recalling the evening. She closed her eyes and relaxed as she tilted her head to the stars. "Speaker, hear me, please, your child."

"Of course, my child."

"I need your guidance, what you will give me. You have sent me to a world that ought to have received a World Walker eighty years ago. I know not your Will, but an Oediohs walked these halls. I do not understand how you could allow that.

Though I know you cannot give me a true answer, I still wish to ask."

"There are many factors I consider before sending one of your kin. For instance, a World Walker had appeared not three years before to defend against a dragon threat, had it not? If I send World Walkers for every threat, then mortals will become reliant on your aid instead of being brave enough to fight for themselves."

"But, Speaker, this was an Oediohs. I cannot think of a threat more dire."

Silence.

"In time, perhaps you will find the answer to your questions. I understand the desire to know more now, but if you learned everything at once, would you be able to view all that knowledge in its kindest light?"

Kan'sa sighed. "Perhaps not. You are

saying that I must find and understand the circumstances more before I will find my answers?"

"Yes, my child."

"Where should I go now?"

"What does your heart say?"

"I would like to visit Hanmark. I believe the Blessed may help me understand some of your cryptic statements."

The voice laughed a jolly, deep laugh. "Perhaps she may. I will watch over you, my child."

"Thank you for your guidance, Speaker."

WORD WALKERS
WILL RETURN.

BOOK 2:
HARTS ON HIGH

COMING SOON